MALLORCA VENDETTA

A Lucas Martell Novel

WILLIAM JACK STEPHENS

Sterling Adventure Group, LLC

Series News

Mallorca Vendetta is the first book of the new Lucas Martell Series.

Book 2, *Emissary of Vengeance*, will be released in October of 2019. Everyone on my mailing list will receive advanced notice of discounts!

Make sure you are on my **Mailing List** when the discounts are announced!.

Get connected with me here: **Mailing List Sign Up**

Or at my website: www.williamjackstephens.com

Prologue

There is another world that lurks behind this world. A world where whims and wishes, fantasies, fetishes, and the most vile desires are all possible for those who can afford it.

Chapter One

T hey were coming ashore at 3:00 a.m. in crashing surf, driven by the constant summer winds that howled along the Algerian coastline. The crescent moon hung fittingly over the Strait of Gibraltar to the west, and the water that was normally deep green in the sun was as black as the night above. Only the faint sparkling starlight reflecting on the spray of the wave caps gave the men any anticipation of the rolling sea beneath the inflatable zodiac.

The conditions weren't ideal to make a night landing in this area with its rocky coastline. To reach the sandy shore in pitch darkness, they had to navigate their way through rocks as sharp as razors. If the zodiac was damaged on the way in, they'd have to trek through the coastal desert terrain sixteen kilometers to their secondary evacuation point. But they would worry about that later; first things first. The most important thing at the moment was to get ashore, and make a night creep through the dunes to the fishing village that lay just outside the town of Tipasa, on the Mediterranean coast of Algeria.

They were six in all. Four American mercenaries, private security contractors they called themselves, employed by the Fairhope Group. All former military, special operations guys with little hope of a future back home and a taste for dangerous living, only with better pay. After years of serving in the sandbox and surviving into their mid-thirties, they transitioned into the private sector and grew to love it over here. Or, maybe they just forgot what life could be like outside the boundaries of war and killing. They couldn't envision anything else. They had no plans or training to do anything else, and the life takes a hold of you after a while; they'd spent too much time down-range. Both in-station and out on mission, they did whatever they wanted with little concern for the brutality or depravity; they no longer navigated with the same moral compass as the rest of the world. They were like hired gunslingers in the old wild west, only in the modern Middle East.

The contractors were hired by the mysterious Fairhope Group to guard the "primary" on this mission, and he was just as big a mystery. The team had come across from the coast of Spain on a reconnaissance vessel posing as a merchant ship, and he never left his cabin until they roped down to the zodiac in the middle of the night. They didn't know his name or who he worked for, and they were instructed by headquarters not to address him directly. They had mission orders for the entry, egress, and a basic idea of what their objective was and nothing more. When the primary chose to give them instructions, they followed his orders; quickly and without question.

He was tall, slender, and dressed in a unique style of desert camouflage they couldn't identify, but they all reckoned he was a weathered old government field agent. Probably from the Central Intelligence Agency originally, but the objective of this mission put him outside the normal scope of the agency's work. He remained completely stoic and silent, not even a throat clearing, during the entire three-hour zodiac run in the dark.

The agent had to be in his late sixties, and from what they could see of his painted face in the starlight, he had the appearance of a man who'd survived more than one suicide mission. A cold, blank stare, and eyes that constantly scanned the horizon in the darkness as if he were looking through infrared. Physically, he was as hard as a coffin nail. Lean, trim, arms like flexible steel cables, and he wore an old elephant-hair bracelet on his left wrist, which meant he probably got his "agency button" in the killing fields of Laos or Cambodia in the seventies. He was an old school bone breaker you didn't want to lie to.

At twenty-nine years of age, the youngest member of the team was also the only one not directly employed by Fairhope Group. He was on loan from the French Foreign Legion. The French government had hundreds of years of history and financial interests all over the North African coast as well as the interior of Africa, and Lucas Martell had served in almost every scorching hell hole where the Legion had a presence. In recent years he was assigned to work with both American and British special operations teams that roamed in remote areas of Afghanistan, capturing and interrogating Taliban insurgents. In addition to his native Spanish, he spoke English, three dialects of Arabic and French, which was widely spoken in this part of Algeria. Just one of the reasons he was selected for this assignment. The other was his talent for killing. At close range or from a great distance, he delivered lethal rounds like they were given guidance from the shooting gods. He never missed. Lucas had also witnessed more than one enhanced interrogation, and had a strong stomach for it.

But Lucas' reputation among his normal military comrades meant absolutely nothing in this team of mercenaries. They regarded him like a stray dog that might be useful for a time to bark at danger in the night, but if they needed to dump him along the trail, or got tired of having to take care of him and just wanted to put him down, no problem. They'd bleed him, and leave him. Never give it a second thought.

LUCAS WAS LYING flat over the starboard front pontoon of the zodiac with his M110 sniper rifle trained forward. Through the night-vision device clipped on the barrel ahead of his scope, he could see the shadowy outline of the Algerian hills floating up and down where they blotted out the stars to the south, and he could hear the faint echoes of the sea as it broke itself against the rocks ahead, in the blackness. He raised and lowered his hand to signal the engine operator in the stern to slow the pace, and be ready to move left or right to avoid the rocks. Lucas had spent his younger years growing up by the sea; school months in Barcelona, and the rest of the year on the beautiful island of Mallorca, Spain. Even in the dark of night he could tell how far they were from the shore and what obstacles lay ahead by the sounds of the water and wind as they met terrestrial surfaces. The sea spoke to him, as did other voices from the dark, but he tried not to think about those.

In the midst of the rhythmic thundering surf in the distance, Lucas began to hear random chaotic crashes and echoes. He suddenly raised his hand vertical and clenched his fist, and the operator instantly twisted the throttle back on the Honda four-stroke outboard engine. The zodiac rocked forward and coasted in near silence, with only the swishing of water and the light *putt-putt-putt* of the idling engine. Lucas raised his head and closed his eyes, turning left, then right to listen and triangulate the water sounds. At once he signaled with his hand for full power to the left, "Hard to port, full power!" he barked.

The operator twisted the throttle wide open and pivoted the engine lever, and the small boat wheeled to the left and leaped forward. An instant later, a massive rock grazed the right side of the boat with a dull screech against the thick rubber, and it revealed itself in the darkness only as the silver spray from the boat splashed against it.

Lucas yelled again, "Quarter-turn to starboard, then full power straight ahead!"

The Fairhope contractor lying out across the opposite pontoon glared at Lucas and brought his finger to his lips, "Keep your voice down, asshole!" he whispered in a hoarse grunt.

The shoreline suddenly appeared in front of the team, the wave caps glowing silver as they broke on the beach, and the engine operator powered straight forward; but Lucas was signaling again to slow down.

"Shore straight ahead, go for it!" the contractor in the bow said to his teammate on the engine.

Lucas was frantically waving his hand to stop, but it was too late. Thirty meters from the beach, the bow of the zodiac suddenly folded inward as they slammed into a massive rock head-on, and the boat bounced like a rubber ball being kicked into the night sky. The engine started to cavitate and the sharp propeller blade roared as it left the water and spun wildly in the air. The boat cartwheeled upward and over its bow and sent all six men and their gear flying into the black night.

Lucas and three of the contractors were pitched low and cleared the rocks, then came splashing down into the surf. The breaking waves picked them up and crashed them down again below the surface, over and over, with barely a moment to gasp for a breath before being buried by the next wave. But in less than a minute they found the sandy bottom was under their boots and they could kick upward to keep their heads above water, and slowly work their way to the beach. They instinctively clung to their weapons despite the pounding waves and near drowning.

The primary agent was sitting next to the engine operator in the back of the boat, and both of them were sent flying in a more upward trajectory. The old man flew slightly to the right, and came down along the shallow outside of the rock that had upended the boat. It was covered with moss and seaweed, and though he hit with a hard thump, it cushioned his fall and he slid gently into the water. He swam forward to the beach without ever losing his composure or his stoic stare.

The engine operator wasn't as lucky. He summersaulted in the air and fell straight down onto the jagged peak of the rock, and his spine made a loud crunch that could be heard over the noisy sea. The air in his lungs burst out in a cough, and he flopped helplessly into the water. He made one feeble attempt to paddle with his left arm, then his heavy gear dragged him down beneath the waves. He never resurfaced.

The three Fairhope men all came ashore at the same time, dropped to the sand to catch their breath for a moment, then took up defensive firing positions. Lucas waded in until he was waist deep, then stopped to turn and search the water for the other two who had been in the back of the boat. He watched and listened, then heard the clear splashing rhythm of a swimming stroke over the waves. As the old agent came in close, Lucas reached and grabbed him under the armpit, and helped him get his footing, and the man waded ashore from there.

"Where's Chief Davis, is he coming behind you?" one of the contractors asked.

"I heard him hit the rock, and it sounded like a terminal impact. He's gone," the old man answered.

"He's not gone! We're not leaving until we get him out of the water!"

The old agent slid forward and for the first time, stared directly into the man's eyes with a look that penetrated the darkness, "I said he's gone, and we move out now. Don't ever make me repeat myself again."

The three contractors turned around and came shoulder to shoulder, automatic weapons held in front and angled down. They flipped up their night-vision goggles, looked at the agent, and then looked at Lucas as he came splashing out of the surf.

"This was your fault, asshole!" one said.

Lucas stood straight, his sniper rifle now slung across his shoulder, and his hand hanging to his side just below the .40 caliber pistol on his belt. He didn't make any sudden moves, but he was watching the waistlines of the three men. Their belt buckles would be the first thing to move if they went ballistic. He stood silently, waiting.

"Stand down, soldier," the agent growled.

The tense facedown lasted another twenty seconds, before the three relented and began to tend to their gear. Lucas let out the breath he'd been clenching, tapped the grip of his pistol for reassurance, and turned back to face the sea.

They checked their weapons and inventoried ammunition and what equipment had been attached to their gear belts, which was all they had left now. Thankfully, they still had the GPS navigator and could pinpoint their exact location and plot a course to their objective. The mission was still a go. They took a quick reading before turning southeast into the desert dunes.

Even in the early morning hours, the air was thick and hot, barely dropping below ninety degrees. Lucas knelt down at the water's edge to wash the sandy grit from his hands, and paused to listen and look across the moonlit water. He'd been posted in places away from the sea for many years, and forgotten how much he missed it. It made him think of her. He wondered what she would look like now, or where she might be; if she were still alive.

Chapter Two

"The Sack Man is in the water. He's coming for you," Lucas said.

His little sister, Eliza, who just turned eleven-years old, was only mildly phased by his taunts. He'd been using the legends of "The Sack Man" to torment her since she was five, but she was nearly past the fear of it. "El Hombre del Saco" was the devilish creature in Spain who captured naughty children in a large sack slung over his shoulder and whisked them away to the depths of hell, never to be seen or heard from again. The Spanish version of the Boogeyman.

"You're lying!" she said, and then she inched further out into the blue-green water of the bay.

She waded carefully out, feeling along through the sand and shells that tickled the bottoms of her feet, until the gentle lapping waves were almost to her neck. She bent her head forward into the sea and opened her eyes. The salt water burned just a little, but she blinked and held her gaze, and then she could see the most marvelous school of little green and yellow fishes swimming in circles around her feet as she buoyantly bounced on her little toes, and the golden sand floated up into a cloud.

She raised her head out of the water in a gasp and whipped her long curly hair to the side, "There's no Sack Man down there, only beautiful fish!" she said. She looked around for Lucas, but he was gone.

And then the attack came. A tight grip on her ankle; a strong jerk, and she was swept off her feet and dragged below the water. She shrieked as she went under.

She opened her eyes again below the water and saw her brother, Lucas, blowing cackling bubbles in his triumphant surprise.

Eliza came flailing to the surface, screaming for help. Her mother, sitting beneath a large umbrella on the ivory sand beach, pulled her Gucci sunglasses down on her nose and tilted her eyes forward to see what misery Lucas was inflicting on his little sister now.

"Mom, he's trying to drown me!" Eliza cried.

"Come out of the water dear. Lucas, stop being such an ass to your little sister."

"I was just playing, Mom. She's such a little baby,"

Lucas answered. Then he turned and breast-stroked further out into the bay, and rolled to float on his back and spirt a stream of water into the air. He was completely unaware that this would be one of the last care-free moments in his existence.

HE LIKED the beaches and the ocean here at their family villa in Mallorca, but it was boring for a seventeen-year-old boy with no friends. The only other teenagers on the island were locals who lived in the city of Palma or in the coastal fishing villages on the other coast. Torturing his sister was all he had to keep himself entertained.

Eliza retreated from the water and came up to her mother's umbrella, flopped on the towel next to her, and sulked. She loved her big brother and she wanted him to be her best friend, but he was always mean to her.

Her mother reached down and rubbed a towel over her hair. Eliza was born with the most amazing long curls the color of freshly pressed honey, and her mother's friends and the rich people who came to parties at their home in Barcelona always admired it. It was a feature that distinguished her more typical Catalonian beauty; the warm, olive complexion of a girl born near the sea with emerald green eyes.

It could have easily been argued that she was among the most beautiful of little girls in the world. Even at eleven, she moved gracefully like her mother; lifting herself merrily on her toes when she was happy, and her thick mane of hair bounced and rolled in waves behind her. She often tried to pull it into a knot to keep it out of her eyes, but her mother preferred it loose, so everyone could admire it.

"Why don't you go back to the villa and take a quick shower and wash the salt from your hair, sweetie. You don't want to damage your beautiful hair."

"Can Lucas come with me?" she asked. Then she called out to her brother, "Lucas, please come with me to the house!"

"He'll be along in a minute Eliza. You go on now," her mother said.

"Ok, Mom," Eliza said. Then she wrapped the thick cotton towel around her waist and skipped up the stone trail to their villa, that was above the beach, and just over the hill.

After a while, Lucas came out of the sea and walked to where his mother was still deeply engrossed in a novel.

"You should be nicer to your sister, Lucas. She's little and she looks up to you," she said.

"Sorry, Mom."

"Why don't you go up to the house and tell her you're sorry, and then get yourself cleaned up. Your father is going to meet us at the house and take us to the beach club for lunch today," she said.

Lucas pulled his towel up from the sand and shook it out, then flung it over his shoulder and walked across the shoreline to the trail, keeping his feet in the edge of the water to avoid the scalding white sand.

He was a tall, chubby teenage boy on the cusp of developing into a handsome young man. His dark wavy hair shined as if wet, even when dry, and fell into place with a shake and a stroke of his hand, appearing disheveled only when it was combed. He was athletic, but his pampered lifestyle kept him heavy and awkward, and his mother constantly babied him and pushed sweets and treats on him. It made her happy to feed him, because she was rarely around to raise him. She had many other obligations, being the wife of an important financier, and most of her true affection was reserved for Eliza.

Lucas' father, Francisco Martell, was an investment banker, and a very successful one. He worked for a private equity firm based in Monaco, and traveled frequently between the home office and their clients' offices, many of whom were wealthy Middle Easterners. He spent time in Algiers, Cairo, and Dubai nearly every month. He kept his family living in Barcelona because of the private schools and central location, but they came to spend part of the hot, dry summers at their villa on the island of Mallorca, looking out over the Mediterranean Sea.

He was a tall, classically handsome Spaniard who preferred fine clothes and elegant meals; and even though he brought his family to Mallorca every summer, he hated the beach. But, the Balearic Islands were centrally located between Spain, Monaco, Italy, and Algiers; and he could reach any of his regular destinations with a short flight. The villa he purchased, which had the most commanding view of the Mediterranean Sea from the hill above Port d'Andratx, on the west side of the island, was a very good investment, and only fifteen minutes from the capital city of Palma.

Lucas veered off the stone path that led directly to their villa, and walked instead on the gravel trail that had a better view of the beach below. There were always beautiful woman on the beach this time of year. Some resting below shaded canopies or umbrellas to protect their delicate skin, and others wearing swimwear that left little to the imagination of a seventeen-year old boy. Many of the women would lie on broadly spread towels with their tops removed to evenly tan the breasts, which is a normal part of the Mediterranean culture. But at his age, Lucas often found himself suspended by the sight; unable to control his fascination or his imminent condition.

On this particular day, he paused for several minutes to stare over the cliff, and then pulled the towel from his shoulders and held it loosely in front of his body to hide the evidence of his arousal. He couldn't take his eyes off them. He stood there, lost in his imagination and wondering what it would be like when he finally made love to a woman for the first time. Then, some unknown noise from over the hill, startled him out of his dream. He felt a moment of embarrassment, he looked around to make sure no one was watching him, then he continued on the trail to the villa.

THE MARTELL FAMILY had no way of knowing that, since the break of dawn, they were being watched. A pair of Zeiss binoculars had seen the first lamp in the kitchen window flicker on at 6:00 a.m., and they followed the housekeeper's arrival an hour later. A logbook was noted, and confirmed that the regular patterns were being followed.

At 8:05, slightly behind schedule, Francisco stepped out the front door with his briefcase in hand, leaving for a meeting at the Mallorca National Bank in Palma. He paused as someone called his name; his wife, Loren, stepped out in a celeste blue, satin morning robe. He turned and kissed her left cheek, and then walked briskly to his car in the parking lot down the hill. She watched him walk until he was out of sight, as she always did, then returned to the house.

At precisely 10:00, Lucas and Eliza raced from the front door in their beach clothes and sandals, with towels tucked beneath their arms. They hurried to find a prime spot on the sand, and Loren followed closely behind, wearing a shimmering gold one-piece, with a violet-colored sash around her waist, and a wide hat woven from strips of tropical palm. She carried a large canvas bag on her arm, filled with towels, bronzing oils and zinc cream for her lips, and a new hard-bound novel.

"There she is," a voice whispered into a small hand-held radio.

"We see her," came a reply in his earpiece.

The spotter moved to a new vantage point and maintained his vigil, and almost two hours to the minute later, he radioed another message, "Target is on the move."

"She's solo. Be ready."

"All clear. Take her now."

AFTER LUCAS BROKE AWAY from his lustful staring and continued on to the villa, he passed the driveways that led to other homes that were tucked into private gardens and clusters of trees on the hill. When he reached their house he walked in the front door and called to his little sister.

"Eliza, I'm sorry!"

There was no reply.

"Maybe she's still in the shower," he thought. He

walked down the hallway to the bathroom door and lightly knocked.

"Eliza, are you in there?"

Still no reply.

"Come on, I said I was sorry."

He knocked again, and the door pushed open. He poked his head inside and looked around, but it was empty. He went to her room and found it empty too, and then to every room in the villa, but she was nowhere to be found.

"If you're hiding and trying to scare me, it won't work!" he said loudly. But again, no reply.

He walked out the front door and looked around, then walked down the gravel driveway that led to a parking area on the hill below and the road to the city. The afternoon breeze was beginning to pick up, and a movement caught his eye down the path.

On the edge of the drive, hung in the prickly *retama* shrubs, was Eliza's beach towel, softly swaying in the gentle air. He ran down the drive and pulled the towel from the bushes, and walked further along the road. When he reached the crest of the hill, he looked down to the large parking area and saw two workmen loading a rolled-up carpet into the back of an old blue van.

He wouldn't have normally thought much about it, there were many fine homes here in Mallorca and the rich people liked to have their expensive Persian carpets taken and professionally cleaned. He'd seen it many times before. But there was something else that grabbed his attention. Something funny about that carpet. It was lumpy, not rolled into a smooth, tight tube.

Then he saw something that his brain couldn't quite process. It looked like hair. A long clump of golden curls, dangling from the end of the rolled carpet. He was confused.

LUCAS AND ELIZA had been raised in a world of privilege. A sheltered world. Sheltered from the dangers and evils that lurked around them. It would have never occurred to them that someone might want to harm them. Lucas' mind couldn't process what he was really witnessing; that someone was abducting his little sister.

Still confused, but alarmed, he began to run down the driveway to the van. He yelled at the men as he ran, "Hey! What are you doing? My sister is in that carpet, stop and let her out!"

The men seemed to ignore him and threw the carpet up into the back of the old van and slammed the doors shut. One walked calmly around to the driver's door, climbed in and started it up. The other went to the passenger side and opened the door.

Lucas was closing in on them now, and he yelled again, "Stop, or I'll call the police!"

At that, the man on the passenger side turned and

faced him. He was the same height as Lucas, but thickly built, and outweighed him by thirty pounds. His skin was burnished from the sun, to a dark brown, and he had small, jet black eyes recessed deeply below a protruding brow that was covered in a single row of black hair from one side of his face to the other. He was wearing poor workman's canvas pants, like the ones sea-faring men wear, and a dirty gray tee-shirt that stretched around his solid chest.

Lucas ran straight up to him. He'd never confronted a man before; never had reason, but he was starting to understand what was going on, and he was ready to fight for Eliza. He never saw the punch coming.

His head was spinning, and all he could hear was a deep, throbbing baritone pulse.

His vision was blurred for a moment, and then cleared. He was lying flat on his back in the gravel and looking up at the dark man, who was now drawing a long, rusty blade from behind his back.

"Hey, what's going on there?" someone yelled from the path on the hill above.

The dark man looked up and saw that they were being watched by an older man and woman on the hill, and he turned quickly and jumped into the van. The driver put it in reverse and backed up in a hurry, and Lucas rolled to his right, barely escaping being run over. Then the wheels of the van spun wildly, burying Lucas in gravel and dust as it sped away.

"They have my sister! They took my sister!" he screamed at the top of his lungs.

"Eliza!"

Chapter Three

TIPASA, ALGERIA

L ying face down in the scorching sand, with the ear-piercing whistle of bullets passing inches above his skull, Lucas smiled. He smiled at the warm glow he felt every time someone was trying to kill him. It felt familiar, comforting, and oddly like foreplay. And after all, this is exactly what he signed up for, twelve years ago. He wanted to be thrown into the middle of the worst shit the world could offer. A place where he could prove himself, or die a violent death. Death, he thought, would be the only thing that could recover a shred of his honor. The one thing that would make him ultimately worthy. He secretly longed for it. Dying in battle would bring him redemption from his cowardice and failure. But it couldn't be just any death. It had to be glorious.

Lucas, the old agent from Fairhope Group, and

the three surviving mercenaries had navigated under the cover of darkness through the coastal dunes and desert scrub for six miles. They arrived at their destination, a small group of mud-brick buildings on the outskirts of Tipasa, Algeria; then immediately came under fire as they crested the final hill.

Lucas looked around at the rest of the team, scattered behind rocks or scrub, and one digging his way straight down into the sand like a badger. He made eye contact with the old agent, still cool and emotionless in the middle of a firefight, and the old man gave him instructions with silent hand gestures, "*Two shooters to the north of the compound; take them out when I draw their fire.*"

Lucas nodded his understanding of the order.

He reached up and pulled the top of his olive tee-shirt out far enough to gently wipe the sand from the corners of his eyes, then pulled his sealed combat glasses up from the lanyard. Then he slid off his beret and shook it out before pulling it tightly back on his head and down over the right side of his face, where the afternoon sun was flaring across his rifle scope. He slid the barrel up over his pack, and waited for the agent to make his move.

The agent took his camouflage hat off, lifted it slightly above the lip of the dune with a small stick, and gave it a wiggle. The reaction was instant. Both of the shooters were Tauregs, the desert people of North Africa, and dressed in traditional clothing of life in the open dunes; indigo-dyed wraps and turbans that covered their heads and faces, leaving only a slit for their eyes. They were hunkered down behind an old mud-brick wall, and swung instantly on the hat as it bobbed into sight and opened fire on full auto. The muzzle flashes and cordite smoke blinded them for just an instant, which was all Lucas needed.

He held the scope reticle slightly above center mass on the near-side shooter and punched a hole through the biggest part of him. The impact snapped his head forward and folded his body in two, drove him backward into the air and left him splayed out on the sand like he was making a snow angel. As the smoke cleared and the second Taureg realized he was now standing there alone, he tried to drop quickly to his knees below the wall, but his bright colored turban exploded in a purple-pink mist and his body folded in a heap.

"Clear," Lucas yelled after scanning the other outbuildings and the nearby goat pen through his rifle scope.

The agent stood and spoke directly to the three mercenaries, "You three, clear that other building on the left. Legionnaire, you're with me to the house on the right."

The mercenaries spread out and moved cautiously down the dune, weapons aimed straight at the barn-like structure on the left, and Lucas followed the agent, slinging his sniper rifle and pulling his pistol out for close quarters shooting. They approached the house, the agent moving to the left of the door frame to enter quickly, as Lucas rushed straight ahead and slammed his foot against the door, just below the handle.

As he ran into the room he moved to his right against the wall, pistol aimed forward. The inside was dark and the air swirled with fine desert dust and a dank foul smell, like rotting flesh. His eyes needed a few seconds to adjust from the bright sunshine outside to the unlit cave-like darkness, and he prayed that he wasn't going to face an attacker at that moment. The agent had come in right on his heels and moved to the left, sweeping his pistol left and right for potential threats. He was wearing full wrap around blackened sunglasses, and pulled them down as he entered so his shooting vision was instantly clear.

As the dust settled from the air down to the dirt floor, they saw a figure huddled behind a wooden table against the wall. Lucas barked the order in Arabic, "'Arini Yudik!" (Show me your hands!)

There was no response, the figure stayed huddled down.

He changed effortlessly to French, "Montre moi tes mains!"

They heard a faint whimper, and then an old woman slowly rose to her knees and raised her hands upward. She was ancient, with hazel colored eyes that had the fog of cataracts; weather-desiccated skin and deep wrinkles in her face that resembled the hide of an elephant. And when she opened her mouth to speak, there were only three gray teeth chattering from the bottom jaw against her upper plate. She was terrified, glancing quickly back and forth from Lucas to the agent, then suddenly pointed to the weather beaten door to her left, "Il est dedans!" she screamed, shaking a crooked finger frantically toward the door.

"What's she saying," the agent asked.

"She says, 'He's in there.'"

They both shifted the aim of their weapons away from the old woman and toward the door.

"Who's she talking about? Who's in there?" Lucas asked.

"The man I came to kill."

The agent moved silently, reaching forward with each step and rolling the heels of his desert boots over the silty dirt floor without making a sound. He was gripping his 9mm Glock pistol with two hands, and he eased his left index finger forward over the trigger guard and tapped the On-button of the small laser sight that hung below the barrel. A scalding red dot appeared on the door. Lucas moved close to the door on the right side, and reached down to grasp the handle and throw it open, while the agent positioned himself to enter and fire. Lucas had a firm grip on the handle now, and waited for the signal. The agent, still calm and composed as he had been all day, never took his eyes off the door, he simply nodded, "Now."

The rusty door hinges whined as it flung open, and the agent vanished into the dark room. Lucas stepped around to the entrance, prepared to follow, but there was no need. The room was tiny, barely large enough to hold a small single bunk with a grass-filled mattress. The agent was standing over it, the laser dot shining down on a rotting corpse. The man he'd come to kill was already dead.

Lucas broke the silence, "Who was he?"

"He was a low-level broker. He moved merchandise and handled the money for a few militant groups that needed to be shut down."

"Looks like someone put him out of business already," Lucas said.

"It would appear so. No matter, his laptop was left here in the room untouched. I should still be able to recover some information from it."

Lucas turned to the old woman, "Qu'est-il arrivé?" (What happened?)

The old woman began a frantic rapid-fire babble of broken French and Arabic.

"She says he got into an argument with the Tauregs, the desert people, over some of the merchandise, and they stabbed him. They told her not to go in there, and she swears she hasn't stepped foot through the door for a week," Lucas said.

"It smells like she's telling the truth." Then the agent added, "Ask her about the merchandise."

Lucas turned back to the old woman and spoke in French, "Tell me about the merchandise."

Again the old woman slurred and spit her way through a long diatribe, and pointed her arthritic fingers out the door.

"She says the merchandise is in the animal barn."

Chapter Four

❧

The quiet seaside village of Punta de Manresa is scattered about the north eastern coast of Mallorca. A few old Roman-era ruins and official buildings in the hills above the beaches, a few apartment buildings along the edges of the white sand dunes, and a sizable deep draft marina.

The marina accommodates personal sailing boats and day yachts, and also has a long pier dedicated to seasonal commercial craft, colorfully painted fishing boats mainly, and most in a state of rot from years of use and little care. They visit from other parts of the Mediterranean for supplies, repairs, and ice to keep their fish catch from spoiling before they reach their home port. It's a sleepy little hamlet by the sea where much of nothing happens, and the perfect place to disguise a criminal enterprise.

The old blue van pulled into the little marina and traveled through the main parking area and onto the very end of the gravel camino, to the place where the commercial fishing boats were moored. The driver and the dark-skinned man stepped out, scanned their surroundings briefly, then opened the rear door and pulled the lumpy rolled carpet from the back. They carried the carpet like a tree trunk, each holding one end, and walked the length of the long pier to where an eighteen-foot motor launch waited. The carpet was carefully handed down from the floating dock to two men waiting in the boat, and when it was loaded on the deck they started the engine and headed out of the harbor.

The motor launch cruised at half speed in the midday swells, going up and down with waves and occasionally hitting the bottom trough of the following crest hard enough to rattle the teeth of the men, and cause the faintest of cries to be heard escaping from the carpet roll.

Four miles offshore they came alongside a one-hundred-and-eighty-foot luxury craft, anchored far enough away from shore to feel like a private island of its own. As they pulled up, another crewman on deck tossed a line and they tied it securely to a cleat on the stern. Then they passed the carpet up to the deck and carried it into the lower level of the yacht, the open salon, which was richly decorated with mahogany and teak panels and furniture, and Persian rugs on the wood flooring. They placed it in the center of the room and quickly left.

A man entered the salon from the galley entrance and stood looking down at the carpet, and shook his head in disgust at the barbarism. He was in his early forties, medium height and build, gleaming black hair cropped short and slicked with oil, and with richly browned skin that comes from a life in the North African deserts and along the Mediterranean Sea. He was wearing a beautiful blue silk kaftan robe, embroidered with gold trim.

He knelt down and gently pushed the carpet to unroll it. As it spun across the floor and opened, the young girl came flopping out and gasped for breath. She was dressed only in her pink-striped bathing suit, still mildly damp, and her long golden hair was twisted and frazzled into knots. Her face was blistering red from near suffocation and swollen from crying into the cramped, hot wool rug where she'd been cocooned for the past two hours. She looked up from the floor at the man standing over her, and then looked around at the strange surroundings.

"Where am I?" she said weakly.

The man smiled broadly with huge white teeth and in strongly accented Spanish he said, "You are on your way to a new life."

"I want my mother! Where is my mother?" she cried out.

"Your mother is not here, and you will never see her again. That life is over."

"No! I want to see my mother now! Where is my brother? I heard him calling for me; where is Lucas?"

The smile vanished from the man's face. He reached into his kaftan and pulled a long curved knife with an ebony handle. He grabbed Eliza by the hair and held the edge of the knife against the terrified little girl's neck, "Forget that name, and forget you ever had any family! You will do only what I tell you to do from this moment, or I will send my men back to kill your parents and your brother, too! Do you understand me?" he yelled.

She sat petrified and silent.

He bent closer until his long nose was nearly touching hers, his eyes narrowed and his teeth tightly clenched, "Do you understand!?" he grunted again.

Eliza was unable to speak from fear. She slowly nodded her head.

As he raised his voice, two women came into the salon, both covered from head to foot in black, their faces veiled with only a fine slit across their eyes.

"Take her to the cabin in the front and sedate her. We have a long journey, and she needs to be kept calm. The Sultan will not be pleased if she injures herself before I present her, and then I would have to just sell her at the Bazaar for nothing. She must be perfect and unblemished. When we reach Algiers, have her bathed and prepared for the flight," the man ordered.

The two women nodded silently and quickly pulled Eliza up from the floor and carried her away.

Chapter Five

Lucas and the agent walked outside in the direction of the animal barn, keeping their heads on a swivel in case there were other Tauregs hanging about. The barn was an old building made with bricks composed of mud and grass, and then plastered on the outside with clay, dug from one of the desert fresh-water wells. The walls were two feet thick, and as ugly as they were, they held the desert heat at bay and kept a constant 72 degrees inside.

The walls were also nearly perfectly soundproof, and they didn't hear the first cry until they were reaching for the rope handle latch on the outside of the shuttered door. They drew their guns forward and pushed quickly through the door prepared for trouble, but the scene they walked into marked a turning point for Lucas. A moment that would alter the course of his life.

The first thing they saw as they entered the barn and the sunlight lit up the room from over their shoulders, was the gleaming white ass of one of the men. He was hunched forward and trying to pin down a struggling young girl over a wooden bench. The other two men were also engaged in the act of rape, each having torn the clothing from two other young girls, barely thirteen or fourteen years old by the looks of them. Two more girls, one as young as nine or ten, were curled up on the dirt floor in the corner of the barn, clutching each other and shielding their eyes.

Lucas went mad.

He raced forward to the first man, reached around and seized him by the throat, pulled his head upright and placed the barrel of his pistol against the back of his head. The shot painted the wall red. Lucas moved with deliberate calmness to the second man a few steps away, who was rolling off of his victim and reaching for his weapon, and he fired two rounds rapidly into his chest. The man fell to the ground and rolled to his back, his eyes filled with panic as his mouth opened and sucked frantically for breath like a perch pulled from the water, but his lungs were shattered.

Lucas stood over him, looking down into his eyes with raw hatred. A hate he hadn't felt welling inside him since he was a boy. He pointed the muzzle of his pistol at the tip of the man's nose and waited until he saw it in his eyes; the realization his life was about to end. He pulled the trigger, and then kept pulling it until the magazine was empty.

Lucas was standing over the bloody mess at his feet, the pistol still pointed downward and the slide of the gun locked back exposing the empty chamber, when he heard the roar of the Glock behind him. The agent had taken out the third man, who by then was drawing to fire at Lucas from across the room. Two quick shots to the chest, followed by a precision third to the head. A technique commonly called the "*Mozambique*" by old school killers.

"You're not going to live very long if you lose situational awareness, boy," the agent said. "If you're not shooting, you're reloading. If you're not reloading, you're moving. And if you're not moving, you're dying."

LUCAS REGAINED HIS COMPOSURE. He ejected the spent magazine with the thumb of his gun hand, and swiftly pulled a fresh magazine from his belt and slipped it into the handle of the pistol. Then he levered the slide release to chamber a new round with a snap. He looked around the room at the carnage, and then realized that the five young girls were as terrified by him as they had been by the men who were savaging them before.

He slowly holstered his weapon, and held his open hands out in front of him. "Don't be afraid. We won't hurt you," he said in French. All five girls were now huddled together in the corner, shivering uncontrollably and weeping. His words had no comforting effect on them. He spoke again in French, "I'm going to help you, no one else is going to hurt you, I promise." But again, they didn't seem to understand. They looked at each other as if they were hearing a completely foreign language.

Then the oldest girl spoke with a quavering voice in Spanish, "Please don't hurt us anymore."

Lucas was startled. Spanish wasn't a language normally spoken this far into the North African territories. He switched immediately to his native tongue, "We won't hurt you! We are here to help."

Then he bent down to one knee, as he might have done to seem less intimidating to a frightened little creature on the streets, and held out his hand to her. He offered a smile and beckoned her forward. The girl looked into his bright green eyes, hesitated for just an instant, and then rushed forward and flung herself into his arms. He held her close and gently stroked her hair with his hand, "It's going to be ok, you're safe now." A moment later, all five little girls were clinging to Lucas in a pile, and crying aloud.

When the girls were calmed, Lucas started asking

where they were all from, and how they came to be here, even though the answers to his questions were already ringing in his mind. He knew exactly what had happened to them. Most of them, it turned out, came from small towns at the tip of Andalusia, and had been kidnapped from the streets or even from their own homes in the night, and smuggled by various means across the Strait of Gibraltar into Morocco.

They had no idea how long ago they had been taken, but they had been moved from place to place by truck, every few days. They weren't sure how long they had been here in this barn, but it had felt like a long time. The old woman came daily with a bucket of dirty water and a few loafs of crusty Arabic bread, and that was all they had to eat. If they cried or made noise, the old woman came back with a stick and beat them, and in recent days the dirty men wrapped in dark blue rags had come to look at them many times.

The littlest of the girls held the most painful news for Lucas. As she warmed to his smile and began to shyly answer his questions, she told him that she was from a small village outside the capital city of Palma, on the island of Mallorca; Lucas' home. Her nightmare had begun in the same place and much the same way that Lucas had started his own journey to hell, nearly twelve years before.

"Not to spoil the party, but what do you plan to do now? We have no boat, and you've managed to kill the men who were supposed to keep me alive until I make it out of this shit country," the agent said. "I see you've got a soft spot for little girls, but we can't take them with us."

Lucas looked up at the old man with a fierce gaze, "I'm not leaving them behind."

The old man had interrogated enough people in his years to know the truth when he heard it, and believed him. He believed Lucas would give his life at this moment to protect them. He thought carefully before he spoke again, "Alright. You gather a few more weapons and all of the ammunition you can carry from the dearly departed. The girls will have to walk on their own, and keep up. If they fall behind, I keep walking. I'll go see if the old woman has any food and water. We've got to make the secondary evacuation point by 6:00 a.m., or swim back to Spain."

"We'll make it," Lucas said.

In ten minutes Lucas had the girls gathered in a line outside the barn. He was loaded with three additional weapons besides his sniper rifle and pistol, and the two oldest girls were carrying ammunition belts over their shoulders.

They heard a muffled pop come from inside the house, and then the agent emerged with a sack full of bread and a large water bag. "The old woman said the Tauregs had gone off early this morning, on horses. They were headed to the wellspring and they will be returning soon. We need to leave now and keep walking through the night to stay ahead of them. We have the GPS so we can stay on course, but if we stop during the night, they will be on us by first light."

"What was the noise in the house?" Lucas asked.

"The old woman was quick to point directions; better the Tauregs have to spend some time sorting it out for themselves rather than knowing which way to follow us. And let's face it, she wasn't exactly a model citizen."

THE UNLIKELY GROUP of two killers and five little girls pushed forward through the desert under the cover of stars. Despite his fears about their stamina, the girls stayed faithfully on step and made nary a sound. They had seen much worse in the previous weeks, and this was their only chance at being saved and returned to their families; they weren't going to be left behind.

When the sand was deep and silty and the littlest girl's legs were too short to climb the dunes, Lucas lifted her onto his back and carried her, clinging to his neck. He taught the girls how to rope themselves together into a chain, and he led the group up and over the steep rocky hills, pulling from the front.

At 3:00 a.m., the agent pulled a transmitter from his vest, pointed it skyward, and held down the button for ten seconds. It was silent, but he knew the message was sent. At 5:45, just as an orange glow began to push over the eastern horizon, they crested a dune and looked down on the Mediterranean Sea, and two black zodiac gunboats waiting exactly where they should be.

As THE ZODIACS motored across the windblown sea, out to the ship waiting sixteen miles offshore, Lucas gazed at the northeastern horizon in the direction of Mallorca, lost in his memories of another young girl. Another girl and another time.

The old agent reached over and tapped Lucas on the knee, "Want to tell me what that was all about in the barn?"

Lucas stared into his eyes. They were the deepest black he'd ever seen; almost completely colorless except for a small fleck of gray around the edge. He didn't know how to respond to the question. He'd never lost it like that before. "I don't know what happened…I've never done anything like that before. I mean, I've killed men; but never like that," Lucas said.

"I've spent a lifetime extracting information from people. I can tell by looking at a person whether or not they have secrets or something they're hiding. That looked like pure rage to me," the agent said.

"What's going to happen to me now?" Lucas asked.

"Nothing," the agent said.

"I killed those men. The Legion will execute me if they find out, and I don't think Fairhope Group will be very happy about it either."

"You didn't kill them, the Tauregs did it. We lost a man in the approach; we got to our destination; we were ambushed, and the Tauregs killed the other three. Our target was already dead when we arrived, also killed by the Tauregs. End of story."

Lucas sat looking at him, trying to decide if he could trust the old man and also trying to figure out why he'd be willing to lie for him. No matter how hard he stared, he couldn't get a read on him; he was as blank and emotionless as a stone statue. Never smiled, never frowned, never blinked.

"Who are you?" Lucas asked.

"My name is Diggs."

"Is that Agent Diggs, or Field Officer Diggs?" Lucas asked.

"Just Diggs. I'm an ordinary citizen now."

"There's nothing ordinary about you, Diggs. Who do you work for?"

"It's not so much who I work for now, but what I'm working for. The world might think of me as just a murderer, and that I am, and much worse. But despite my methods, I'm working for redemption. What little I might be able to salvage for myself."

ONCE SAFELY BACK IN his cabin on ship, Diggs opened his laptop computer and logged into a 256-bit encrypted, private network server located in the Seychelles Islands in the Indian Ocean. The server was operated by the Fairhope Group, and all coded communications were completely untraceable and unbreakable. He then signed into a message board, and typed the following:

TIPASA MISSION REPORT - "SUCCESSFUL"

A REPLY CAME: "CANDIDATE EVALUATION?"

DIGGS RESPONDED, "Fieldcraft skillsets are High. Emotionally volatile."

"RECOMMENDATION?"

DIGGS RESPONDED, "Proceed with next phase of evaluation."

Chapter Six

※❀※

In the year that followed Eliza's abduction and disappearance, what remained of the Martell family fell completely apart. The Channel 7 television station in Palma showed pictures of Eliza nearly every night, and positioned a local correspondent and camera crew directly in front of the villa. No one could enter or leave the house without microphones and cameras shoved into their faces and bombarded with questions.

They showed video footage nightly of anyone coming or going from the house, and speculated about the fate of the little girl and who might have taken her. Eventually, Francisco had to remove the television from the house because Loren couldn't stand seeing her daughter's face every time she turned it on.

The *Balearic Diario* newspaper posted a single

reporter to the house as well, but after four weeks had passed without a gruesome discovery or prime suspects being identified, they sent the reporter somewhere else. The readership boost from the kidnapping story began to dwindle, and the world lost interest.

The local police gathered statements and leads, but there was no evidence at the scene of the crime other than the beach towel, and it held no clues besides a few strands of Eliza's long curly hair. The gravel parking lot offered no clear tire tracks or footprints, and no fingerprints other than those of the family were found in the house.

They all waited nervously within reach of the telephone, believing a call would surely come for a ransom; after all, Francisco was a man of means, and what other reason could there be for taking his daughter. He had no enemies that he could think of, in fact the only people he came in contact with were wealthy clients, and he made millions for them, so they loved him. In his mind, it could only be a kidnapping with ransom as the motive.

The older couple on the hill gave a reasonable description of the van, but they argued over the precise color. The man swore it was dark green with a hint of metallic sparkle; and his wife furiously defended her description of a black vehicle with some kind of business logo painted on the side.

Even though they both saw a dark-skinned man

hit Lucas and then climb into the van that sped away, they didn't actually see the carpet roll being loaded into it, so Lucas' word was all the police had to go on. And in truth, he never actually saw Eliza, only what he believed to be a lock of her hair hanging from the carpet. The police grilled him over and over for hours, until he started to doubt what he really saw.

Then the whispers and rumors began.

He was a pathological liar, and fond of telling wild stories for emotional effect.

He was a drug addict, and the punch in the face the couple witnessed was an angry confrontation with his dealer.

And many other wild tales that portrayed him as a troubled young teenager, and perhaps even a closet homosexual who was jealous of his sister's beautiful hair. He was deemed an extremely unreliable witness in the eyes of the world, and likely a boy in need of psychological help.

Then the police pulled his father in and interrogated him for days. For some reason they just couldn't believe that the girl had been abducted. A relative is always the prime suspect in this type of crime. They tried endlessly to force a confession from either Lucas or his father, and when they couldn't get it, they leaked their suspicions to the media.

The failure of the police to solve the crime was ignored, and the family was prosecuted by the vulturous tabloids. They published photographs of the family, altered to make them appear ugly and angry; and any crazy speculation cast by a passing tourist on the beach made for a new headline.

Lucas' mother, Loren, withdrew into her bedroom and rarely left. She pulled the heavy brown shades closed to block out the scorching sun, and spent her days curled up on a lounge chair. She wore the same clothes that she slept in most days, and came out of the room only to use the bathroom or come briefly to the kitchen for something to eat, and to refill her glass with sherry.

Over the weeks and months that followed, the room took on the pungent stench of soiled bedsheets, unwashed clothes and oily flesh. It began to approximate the odor of a decaying corpse, even though Loren continued to suffer with the living.

She stumbled into the kitchen one morning when Lucas was eating his breakfast, and stood and stared at him. There was nothing left in her eyes. No happiness, no sadness, no understanding of the world. Life had completely left her, her body just didn't know it yet. She held lightly to the hope that Eliza would someday come home, and that she should be there waiting for her.

She would never leave the house again; at least, not alive.

Francisco Martell fought with the local police, and then elevated his pleas for help through the spiderweb of Spanish politics. Everyone he spoke to told him since he did not receive a ransom request, then in all likelihood Eliza was already dead or never coming home. They couldn't even get Interpol to list Eliza in the Missing Persons Registry until a formal request was presented by the Spanish government official in charge of these matters. By the time that happened, she could have been on the moon.

Francisco refrained from directly blaming Lucas, at least not to his face. But he would drink alone at night in the salon sitting in the pitch darkness, and mutter to himself as the alcohol dulled his senses and loosened his lips.

"If I'd been there I would have killed those bastards with my bare hands…," he said. " A real man would have fought to the death to save her…"

Lucas heard all of his father's drunken rants.

After three months of interrogations, interviews, and meetings with government officials, Francisco retreated back to the only thing that made any sense in his life; his work at Banco Baudin. Traveling back and forth from the house in Barcelona to the corporate offices in Monte Carlo, he spent most nights away. He spoke only briefly to his wife by telephone, but their conversations were little more than a few hollow words connected by long, agonizing silence. He stopped speaking to Lucas completely.

THE WORDS that sting and fester in our hearts the longest, are not those spoken by others; those things they say to wound us, weaken us, or in stupid jest. The words that will haunt us the most are those we've spoken to others that cause them pain or fear. The words that reveal the mean spirit that lives in all of us. We will hear our own hatefulness ringing in our ears for a lifetime.

In the days, weeks and months that passed after Eliza's abduction, Lucas dwelled on the last words he ever said to her, and fell into a pit of guilt. They were nothing but childish taunts, but they haunted him still.

If he hadn't been so mean to her, she might not have ever gone to the house alone.

If he wasn't so weak and afraid he might have been able to save her.

Every night as he lay tossing and turning in bed, his father's words echoed in his skull, "A real man would have fought to the death…"

He also obsessed about why he was late arriving at the house that day, but told no one, and the shame was like slicing open his belly with a dull blade.

Lucas was sent back to Barcelona to finish his final year in secondary school, and spent most of it living in the home alone. The few nights his father came to the house, he would go directly to his study and lock the door behind him. The housekeeper was his only company, and she always prepared him a breakfast before school, and left a meal wrapped on the table for later, but she was afraid to engage him too closely.

He came home in the afternoons, and after the first month he began to remove his shoes at the door and walk in his socks through the foyer and salon, and up the spiraling staircase to his room. The sound of his hard dress shoes clacking over the marble floors and echoing endlessly through the barren space drove him nearly mad.

He spent his nights in solitude, reading books and magazines, and immersed himself in a world of adventure, heroes, and the great wars of past civilizations. He imagined himself as the mighty Hector, slaying hordes of invaders outside the walls of Troy. He was drawn to the escapades of modern warfare and the elite soldiers who hunted their nation's enemies in the darkest corners of the world; completely unfettered by notoriety. The silent, lethal men who kill for nothing more than duty and honor.

At school, he was like a sickly little creature, who was ostracized from the herd. He hovered somewhere on the periphery, in sight of the others, but always alone. The other boys abandoned him for his perceived cowardice. Even though most of them had never thrown a punch in anger, nor been on the receiving end of one themselves, in particular from a grown man, they mocked him as a weakling.

The girls were more suspicious, wondering if everything they had read in the papers and seen on television was true. Perhaps he had killed his little sister in some twisted fit of deviancy. They huddled in groups in the hallways and whispered and giggled as he passed. Even the one girl that he had known since the first grade who was always nice to him, now avoided him like he carried the plague.

In late June, exactly one year from the day Eliza was taken, he made a fateful decision. Using a knife from his mother's fine silver set, he forced open the door to his father's study. He knew the combination to the safe his father had hidden in the floor, under a carpet behind his desk. He needed only a few things; his passport and birth certificate, and a few hundred euros. There was much more there, but he left it and closed the safe door and relocked it.

He called for a taxi, and walked out the front door with a small backpack over his shoulder, containing only the items he liberated from the safe, and two sandwiches made with prosciutto and slices of Ibores cheese. The taxi arrived a few minutes later, and took him down the long straight Avenue La Rambla until it intersected with the rotonda at Passeig de Colom at the sea shore. He stepped out there and paid the driver, then walked the final mile along the harbor for one last view of the sea, until he arrived at the train station, Estacion de Francia.

He left Barcelona that day on a train bound for Aubagne, France.

His train rolled slowly through the undulating French countryside for the last hour in darkness, and there were only three other passengers in the main car with him, for the final destination. An older couple who sat closely, holding hands and whispering to each other, as they probably had for sixty years; and a young man in his twenties, clean cut and wearing an expensive Parisian raincoat.

The train came to a squealing and steamy stop at the boarding dock in Aubagne. He stepped off, and looked around the station platform, but saw only one young woman waiting under the lamppost, in the humid summer air, with moths and mosquitos flickering above her head in the yellowish light. She looked at him, and then a broad smile opened across her face and she ran toward him.

He had no idea who she was but for an instant, he had the fleeting sensation of being missed and desired, and coming home to family. Then he realized she was running to meet her lover, the young man in the raincoat who stepped off the train directly behind him. She passed him, and leapt into her lover's arms and smothered his face with her warm lips as he swung her in circles.

Lucas turned back to the platform, saw a light on in the small ticket-office window, and approached. An ancient looking man with silver hair sat behind the screen. With his limited high-school French, Lucas spoke, "Monsieur, can you please tell me how to reach the thirteen-thousand block of Quartier Viénot?" he said.

The old man pulled his slender reading spectacles down from his nose and looked at Lucas with a careful gaze, "What business might you have there, young man?"

"Pardon Monsieur, but that business is my own."

The old man snickered, then slid his glasses back in place and resumed reading his paper. Without looking up again he said, "You can take the main road here, through town, past the hospital and the high school, and then as you pass the soccer stadium, go right under the highway overpass. Or, you can follow the train tracks directly down along the highway for two miles, and you'll find what you're looking for on your right. The place you are looking for is well lit at night, you can't miss it."

"I didn't tell you what I'm looking for?" Lucas said, with a puzzled look.

"You're not the first who's come through this station looking for that place, young man. I've seen thousands just like you. Funny, I never see any of them again," he said without ever looking back up.

Lucas chose the dark path along the train tracks, and walked for half an hour along the trail as it paralleled the highway. It was an eerie trail that he would not normally have walked, even in the daylight.

Total darkness, save for a few shadows that cast through the trees from the elevated highway along side it. It was littered with trash, and broken beer and wine bottles, and Lucas tripped and fell twice. It seemed the perfect place that murderers or robbers would likely hide out. He could hear small creatures scurrying about near his feet and into the bushes, like rats or cats or something worse.

Then he saw it. Floodlights lit the outside of the nondescript building. It was rectangular, single story, with a clay tile roof, and low brick walls with iron gates shrouding the entrance. A guardhouse stood by the main gate, with a tall green steel door. A sign on the wall said, LÉGION ÉTRANGÈRE, (FOREIGN LEGION).

At ten o'clock in the evening, Lucas stood before the tall green door and knocked three times. After a few moments without response, he banged three times more with more force. He had read that the Legion recruitment office was open all times of day or night, and he was determined to enlist.

He heard a lock clank and the sliding window next to the door opened to just a crack. A critical hazel-colored eye peered outward and a voice growled, "What do you want?"

"I want to join the Foreign Legion," Lucas answered.

The eye rolled down to inspect his elegant leather shoes, then the dark eyelids squeezed into a cruel slit to scrutinize every detail of him, and slowly scanned his body upward to his head.

"How old are you boy?" the voice asked.

"I turned eighteen two months ago, sir."

Again the eye rolled up and down over him, as if in doubt.

"You'll need to turn over your passport and a birth certificate to prove who you are and your real age, boy."

"Yes, sir. I understand."

"Now boy, you know what you are about to commit yourself to, yes?" the voice asked.

"Yes, sir," Lucas answered. "I have only one request, sir."

"We don't take requests, boy!" the voice barked. "But what might that be?"

"Make me strong and brave."

The eye was silent for a moment, and then responded, "All we can promise you boy, is that we'll make you dangerous; and then we'll find a dangerous place to send you and let you prove how brave you can be."

OVER THE NEXT eleven years the French Foreign Legion made good on their promise.

Lucas surrendered himself completely to the idea that he would either become something worthy of manhood, or he would die. In the early years, he really didn't care which. It took only a year for the Legionnaires to reshape him from a soft upper class boy into a lean figure of a man.

His first post was in Chad in central Africa, and then to the United Arab Emirates. The desert heat was even more oppressive than Spain, but it made him hard and taught him to endure the most brutal conditions. He graduated from general Infantry into the special marksman corps and was trained as a sniper, then sent to Operation Sangaris in the Central African Republic.

After the ousting of CAR President, Françoise Bozizé in a coup d'état, the country erupted into chaotic bloodletting between the Christian militias and largely Muslim nationals. In addition, there were militia warlords roaming the countryside, committing atrocities at random. The French government sent in one thousand Legionnaires to bring an end to the violence, and protect the interests of French owned commerce. Lucas was one of them, and it was here that he made his first verified kill.

It happened on a remote, thorn-tangled hillside in the upper valley of the Central African Republic. The Legion had been playing cat-and-mouse with a tribal warlord who was torturing and murdering everyone in the Christian villages of the valley, and cutting off supply roads that supported a French-run oil refinery.

He had been labeled by command as a "target of opportunity". Kill on sight.

Lucas and his training sergeant were inserted by way of a low-altitude parachute jump into the valley on a cloudy night, and made a long creep to a rocky hill overlooking a small tribal village with a Christian Mission. They settled in for a long wait. Three days later, a small convoy of six trucks came racing up the canyon road and into the village. The younger men and a few women of the tribe fled straight up the mountain side, but the very young and old were quickly captured. The warlord emerged from the last truck and strutted into view.

Lucas had been training with the H&K sniper rifle for nine months, and going through field-craft training for nearly the same amount of time. He was eager to see the "pink mist."

As the warlord stepped out of the truck, his sergeant called it out, "Your target is in the red beret, confirm."

"Confirmed, red beret," Lucas said.

"Range, 730 meters. Altitude 73. Zero wind. You're already clicked in, no adjustments. Wait for a broadside shot…he's turning…turning…green to fire."

Even with a lengthy silencer mounted on the rifle barrel, it made a considerable bark. The ejection ports kept the heavy rifle in line and it recoiled straight back into his shoulder, so Lucas was able to watch the target clearly through the 20X scope when the 7.62mm Nato bullet ripped through the warlord's chest.

All snipers anxiously await that first kill. They dream about it. But when it comes, many aren't prepared for the violent carnage created by a high-powered rifle bullet ripping through human flesh. Most are stunned by what they've just done, and vomiting is a common reaction.

But not Lucas. Lucas felt a pins-and-needle tingle begin at his toes, and then it sparked its way up his legs and into his groin, growing into a wave of euphoria. He took a deep breath, his cheeks went flush and a shiver passed through him that frightened him. His sergeant glanced at his face and then whispered, "Martell, are you alright? You look like you just let go in your shorts."

He'd never felt anything like it; it was almost erotic. It was as close as he could remember to the sensation of release when he masturbated as a teenager. The building rush and tempo, and an instant of euphoric blackout. But he hadn't done that in many years. Not since the day Eliza was taken. It was the shame and guilt that had driven him mad.

Whenever he saw a beautiful woman and felt the pang of desire, it was like a dagger piercing his heart. That sensual fixation had been the very thing that held him on the hilltop that day, staring longingly at the women lying on the beach below, with his hand in his shorts. His lust had kept him from being there in the moment that Eliza needed him most. In his mind, it was the root of every horrible thing that had happened to Eliza, to his mother and father, and to him.

LUCAS WAS PROMOTED a year later to the middle rank of Brigadier, and then sent on special attachment duty to Afghanistan.

He demonstrated a particular talent for picking up languages and local dialects, and after his first five-year enlistment was completed, he re-enlisted and was moved into a special counter-terrorism unit that worked in conjunction with Spec Ops teams from around the world. He had finally become one of them. One of the silent, lethal men who operate in the shadows.

Lucas' existence took shape around a single objective; to hunt and kill evil men. He never questioned the concept of evil, but relied on his superiors to define that for him. It made it easier to focus, and focus kept the ghosts of his past at bay. In moments of rest, his mind would always drift back to the last time he saw Eliza, and to the last words he ever spoke to her. He rarely thought of his mother and father, until the day word came that his father had died.

Chapter Seven

MONTE CARLO, MONACO

⚜

Francisco Martell stepped into the back seat of the Mercedes with his cell phone held to his ear, as the chauffeur held the door open, "Yes, I understand. You have three weeks from today to be in place for the action, and you may never get this opportunity again. Don't worry, they will all be there."

He turned to his chauffeur, Antoine, "I need to make a brief stop at the Hotel Chasson, but I don't want to go in through the main lobby. Take me to the north side of the private parking area and I will walk from there. You can wait there with the car, I will only be inside for a few minutes. We have more than enough time for the drive to the restaurant."

"Oui, Monsieur. As you wish," answered his chauffeur.

Monte Carlo was a maze of twisting, but

meticulously maintained roadways. They followed the original hillside and cliff terrain of the rugged Riviera coastline, and every inch of the micro-state was developed with mansions, casinos, hotels, high-rise apartments, and banks. All of the basic requirements of the world's elite.

Any small parcels of real estate not devoted to those were filled with luxury brand retailers. Vittone, Gucci, Bottega Veneta, Saint Laurent, Balenciaga, Brioni, Sergio Rossi, Pomellato, Girard-Perregaux and Ulysse Nardin, and a few new Russian labels trying to infiltrate the high-end markets. Drawing any color credit card other then platinum or black to pay for goods, results in a smirk that labels you among the peasant class.

Antoine followed the Rue Grimaldi around the famous loop used to field the Formula 1 Grand Prix of Monaco, then detoured off onto Avenue Pasteur and past the tropical Freiluft Garten and the hospital dedicated to Princess Grace. The Hotel Chasson lay just inside the border between Monaco and France, on the beneficial tax side of the line.

As instructed, Antoine proceeded to the north end of the private parking area, which bordered the exotic gardens, and parked the long black Mercedes sedan. He then left the driver's side and rushed to the right rear passenger door to open it and assist his passenger with his heavy case.

As he opened the door and held it, Francisco was

busy gathering a few final papers back into his stainless steel briefcase. He left a large, heavy brown leather travel case on the seat, and then stepped out with his steel briefcase safely clasped to his wrist. Antoine stepped forward and leaned into the rear of the car to retrieve the heavy travel case and as he withdrew with it in hand, a solid blunt object struck him cleanly across the throat, shattering his larynx.

The man who struck him deftly caught the heavy case by the handle as it fell from his grasp, and then stood over Antoine for the next two minutes as he lost consciousness and slowly suffocated. It was a clean kill, and done in a manner that left a plausible injury and cause of death for the plan to follow. The assassin then tapped the end of the steel baton against the roof of the car, collapsed it down into the solid handle, and slipped it into his front trouser pocket.

Antoine's tall, slender frame was folded neatly into the rear luggage compartment, in a somewhat sadistic spooning pose with the other body. They were cozy strangers in death, and essential pawns sacrificed for the master plan.

EYE WITNESS ACCOUNTS of the accident were all very consistent, and as such, it required only vague follow through by the local constable in the small French Riviera village of Cap-d'Ail, which lies on the rugged coast just outside the jurisdiction of Monaco. A Mercedes Benz C500 sedan officially under lease by Banco Baudin of Monte Carlo, had been traveling west along the narrow winding ribbon of Avenue des Douaniers en route to a particularly famous restaurant known for authentic French fare and a wine cave stocked with rare vintage Pinot Noir.

A local woman named Agnes, eighty-seven years of age as she was quite happy to share, who lived in the same cottage house along the Avenue that she was born in, had witnessed the black Mercedes traveling at a ferocious speed past her front window. She sat in a French chair from the seventeenth century in front of her window every evening to watch the occasional elegant car that might come past. She had heard that the President of France was very fond of the restaurant in Cap-d'Ail, and she was certain she would get a glimpse of him one day.

What she saw and heard this particular evening was the speeding Mercedes passing mere feet from her front garden walkway, followed by screeching tires and a thunderous bang, then again by the continued sounds of the car as it smashed its way down the mountainside. She rushed outside, because she is still very spry for her age, peered over the stone wall that borders the edge of the roadway and saw the remains of the Mercedes smoldering and beginning to burn three-hundred feet below at the bottom of the ravine. Agnes then returned quickly to her home and dialed up the local constable, who also happens to be her cousin, Clément.

Within the matter of only a single day, Constable Clément was able to ascertain that the Mercedes was leased to Banco Baudin, and that the regular chauffeur, Antoine, had been assigned to drive Monsieur Francisco Martell, a Banco Baudin executive, to the restaurant for a client meeting that same evening. Antoine had been easy to identify because his body was thrown from the spinning Mercedes and landed away from the vehicle, halfway down the ravine. He had a few scrapes and lacerations, but his death was obviously caused by the steering wheel of the vehicle impacting his throat. He was not wearing his seatbelt and was cleanly ejected from the car as it tumbled over and over down the cliff.

The passenger, Monsieur Martell, had been trapped in the rear seat of the car and was ultimately consumed by the flames. But, since he was registered as the passenger that night, and Agnes positively identified both the chauffeur as a tall slender man and the passenger in the back seat from photographs offered by Banco Baudin, and shown to her by her cousin, Clément, then it had to be Monsieur Martell. Agnes' eyesight is still quite perfect as well, and she swore to it in a written statement.

The news of Francisco Martell's death made only a passing headline in the local six-page Villa Gazette.

The law firm of Charpentier & Boucher, which represented him in most of his personal legal matters, was notified by his employer, the President of Banco Baudin, and his last Will and Testament was activated.

Through two handwritten letters discovered in his desk at the office in Monte Carlo, it was believed that his sole surviving heir, Lucas Martell, was enlisted and on deployment somewhere in Africa with the French Foreign Legion. A message was sent to the regional headquarters to assist in locating Lucas, informing him of his father's passing, and who to contact for details of the funeral arrangements and dispersion of assets.

Chapter Eight

THE VILLA IN MALLORCA, SPAIN

Two days after the secret mission on the Algerian coast as a scout for the Fairhope Group, which ended with Lucas murdering two mercenaries and rescuing five little girls; he arrived at the airborne regiment of the Foreign Legion's Camp Raffalli, near the town of Calvi on the island of Corsica. As he walked into his barracks, a young lieutenant handed him a sealed envelope, "This came for you yesterday. Looks like it's from a lawyer."

The envelope was from the office of Maître Charpentier in Monte Carlo, and was addressed : Monsieur Lucas Martell, Légion Étrangère. There was no Legion base or location on the address, so whoever sent it knew only that Lucas was in the Legion. The postal service at Headquarters had done a remarkably uncharacteristic job of locating him to receive it.

He walked through the long green hallway of the barracks and arrived at the room he had once shared with his sniper teammate, Serge, who had left the Legion the previous year under dubious circumstances. He entered, let his heavy duffel bag slide from his square shoulders to the floor, laid his rifle scabbard carefully on the unoccupied bed, and sat on his to open the letter.

It read as follows:

MONSIEUR MARTELL,

IT IS with deep sorrow that I must inform you of your father's passing. Francisco Martell was a passenger in a limousine that crashed on the outskirts of Cap-d'Ail along the French Riviera on the twenty-third of May this year. All occupants of the vehicle were killed. The exact circumstances of the accident remain undetermined; however, I believe it warrants further investigation.

I was Francisco Martell's personal attorney, and the executor of his Will. There are many details that now require your attention. At your earliest convenience, please arrive at my office in Monte Carlo, that we may complete the required documents and asset transfers, and discuss other issues related to your father's passing.

.   .   .

With Regard,
    Maître Jean-Paul Charpentier

THE NEWS STRUCK Lucas harder than he might have imagined. Even though he hadn't thought of his father much over the years, and their last words were anything but loving, he still harbored a son's instinctive desire to make his father proud of him. His re-enlistment in the Legion was due in three more days, and he had to make a decision; completely abandon his past, or return to the world.

Lucas realized that he had accomplished everything he sought when he joined the Legion. He was not the weak boy he once was, and he feared no one. He was a decorated warrior, and he had taken many lives in the service of something greater than himself. He had nothing left to prove in the Legion. It was time he moved on to something else, and perhaps be someone else who could bring pride to the Martell name. He resigned from the Legion and made plans to travel north to Monaco.

He had no desire to visit the empty crypt of a home in Barcelona, but for some reason he couldn't quite explain, he wanted to be in Mallorca one more time before he attended to his father's funeral. It was a place he loved, and at the same time, a demon that he feared. He had to face it before he could face his father's last wishes.

AS HE LOOKED out the window, there was nothing but azure blue below the Iberia 737, stretching as far as the eye could see. Only a few faint white-caps from the eastern breeze revealed the surface of the water. The plane quivered and thumped as the landing-gear doors unfolded, and the giant wheels levered out into the wind stream. The water drew nearer and nearer as if they were about to ditch into the sea. Then at once, the rocky shoreline passed below the wings, and immediately afterwards the runway lights of the international airport in the capital city of Palma. The tires chirped and smoked as they touched the tarmac, and then the hard braking shifted him slightly forward against the seatbelt. He reached up and braced himself against the seat in front, and then glanced out the window. Lucas was back on the island of Mallorca for the first time in nearly twelve years.

He didn't really know what had drawn him back to this place, only that he needed to be here. He might decide to just sell the villa, he thought. Turn it over to an agent and wait for the money to roll into his bank account. It was a prime vacation home in a playground of the rich. He hadn't decided yet. All he knew is that he needed to come back here before he made a decision.

Lucas rented a little Fiat 500 at the airport and drove slowly along the Ma-19, looking out over the sandy coast of Platja de Palma and Cala Gambia, before he came into the city center. Palma is a modern city with the feel of a medieval tourist town. Many of the side streets that jut off the main avenue are walking streets; solid cut stone underfoot and lined on both sides with four-hundred year old buildings of hand-laid stone and lime plaster, painted a light-absorbing beige. Bright red awnings hang out over the small entry doors to shops, hotels, and bars. Cafes with marble tables on the sidewalks and wide umbrellas to sit under and drink wine in the shade; and clay pots with sego palms and bougainvillea.

It was quiet for a big city, more quiet than he remembered from his childhood. He passed the grand La Seu Cathedral on the waterfront that looks out over the harbor. Started in 1229 by King James the first, and built in the rare Catalan Gothic style, it took nearly four-hundred years to complete, and stands more than thirty feet taller than the famed cathedral of Notre Dame in Paris. Lucas passed by with barely a glance, then took the next narrow brick-paved side street. He came to the road that wound back and forth up the mountain and along the high cliffs to Port d'Andratx, where the villa sat on the hill looking out over the bay.

He caught glimpses here and there of the endless horizon, as he rounded the corners. He pulled over into a sandy lot to see the crystal beaches of Camp de Mar. It was a long narrow inlet where the waves are gin clear at the shore, then fade to strengthening shades of turquoise. Where the water fell to sea depth at the mouth of the bay it transitioned to a rich cobalt blue. The only thing more blue than the sky above was the deep blue sea that surrounded the island.

He'd spent most of the last twelve years in dreadfully stark and violent landscapes, and completely forgot how stunning this little island paradise in the Mediterranean was. For so many years it had always felt peaceful and calm; a safe haven away from the bustling resorts along the mainland shores. The locals were friendly, and the tourists and seasonal residents came seeking serenity, rather than nightlife and noise. It was the most tranquil place in the world, until the day she was taken.

He drove up the road from the little tourist village of Port d'Andratx and wound up the hill through the forest of Aleppo pines, and then suddenly, he was there. He pulled into the leveled gravel parking lot below the homes on the hill.

The memories hit him like a hammer blow.

Twelve years of trying to forget evaporated in an instant. He was once again that seventeen-year old boy lying helplessly in the dirt as he watched his little sister being taken away.

He parked and sat in the car, staring straight ahead into the afternoon sky, his sweaty hands slowly wrenching and squeaking the leather steering wheel as he gathered his nerve. The air was calm and quiet when he stepped out, his sandals crunching over the gravel was the only sound on the hillside as he walked across the lot. His racing heart was pounding out the same fierce baritone drumming in his head that he heard the last time he was here.

He paused and looked at the place where the shitty blue van had been parked. He could see every detail of it in his mind, every scratch and rusty spot; and he could see the face of the dark-skinned man as if he were standing in front of him. He could pick him from a crowd at this very moment. Then he imagined the van spinning its tires and casting a cloud of dust into the air as it left, and felt the stomach-turning sickness all over again.

Eliza was gone, and he couldn't do anything to save her.

THE HIGH VACATION season in Mallorca was just beginning, but most of the homes on the hill were still empty. Lucas' rental car sat alone as he walked up the hill to the villa. It was exactly as he remembered it, a stylish Spanish cottage perched on the hill, with a commanding view of the sea.

At the top of the hill, the thick salty air was replaced with fresh cool breezes from the west, that made the pines whistle and sway. They were ancient trees, rooted in rocks and fissures, and grew slowly over the centuries. Sometimes, even when the wind was still, you could hear the island moving beneath them, as the roots and trunks would creak and groan.

He noticed that someone had been taking care of the house because the garden and walkways were immaculate.

He placed his fingers over the long wrought-iron lever on the front door and pressed down, but it held firm. He'd never known the door to be locked, and he did it purely from habit. He wondered if the key was still resting in its hiding place, or if he would have to break a window. He knelt down beside the walkway and turned over the mossy green stone, and there it was, waiting to be used for the first time.

Eliza had chosen the pretty stone to hide it under, because it was the same color as both her and Lucas' eyes.

He opened the door and walked into the house, and was surprised again to see how clean the interior was, and the shades were open to allow the morning sun to warm it. Was someone living here?

"Hola?" came a call from the front door behind him.

Lucas turned to see a woman standing in the doorway. Middle-aged, pretty, with black hair braided into a long cord that hung forward over her shoulder. She was wearing a typical house-keeper's uniform, and holding a large tray with a dark green cloth draped over it.

Then he recognized her. It was Louisa, the same woman who had cared for the home for many years.

"Louisa? I never thought you would still be here. Actually, I wasn't sure if anyone had been in the house for years."

"Señor Lucas? Is it really you?" she said. She remembered him as a pudgy young boy, but standing in front of her was a chiseled man. She looked pleased.

"Where have you been all these years, and what have you been doing? Your skin is baked from the sun, and your body is…something completely different than it was before. If it wasn't for your beautiful green eyes, I wouldn't know you."

"Yes, it's me," Lucas answered. "I've been gone a long time. Most of it spent in Africa."

"A man came from the city yesterday and told us that you were coming to see the house. I've been keeping it cleaned and ready in case you or your father ever came back for the summer; and my husband has been keeping the garden."

"I can see that. Thank you, Louisa."

She moved into the kitchen and put the tray down on the table, "I brought some tapas for you. There isn't any food here, and I thought you might be hungry after a long journey. There's wine in the cellar, would you like me to bring one up for you?" she asked.

"I'll fetch one later, Louisa. Thank you for the tapas."

She started to walk towards the door, and then suddenly turned and came to him and wrapped her arms around him, "It is so wonderful to see you again, Lucas. We thought we had lost you both so long ago." She paused, and looked into his eyes, "We think about her often." Then she left and closed the door behind her.

Lucas walked through the house, stopping to look into each room. He went into his parents' bedroom, and found the shades opened and the room filled with warm light. It looked very different from the last time he'd seen it, with his mother curled tightly in a ball on the lounge, wrapped in a shawl. He walked into the master bathroom and stood staring at the elegant porcelain tub that stood on gold-leafed claw feet. That was where his mother had taken her last breath.

A few months after he was sent back to Barcelona, his mother reached the end. She drew a tub full of warm water, swallowed a bottle of tranquilizers with Perrier, and slipped into the tub.

He walked back out into the long hallway and looked into his old room, and then turned and stared at the last door. The door to Eliza's bedroom. He reached for the door handle, and then stopped and pulled his hand back as if he almost touched something hot.

This was the only room he wasn't yet ready to see.

Chapter Nine

THE VILLA

The next morning, Louisa came early to make breakfast and found Lucas standing at the end of the hallway, staring intently at the door as if he were bracing himself; preparing to enter a place charged with emotion, and rife with danger.

"I've been keeping it cleaned, Lucas. And nothing has been moved, it's just like it was when she,…when she left us."

He looked up, and she could see the fear in his eyes. Eliza wasn't going to be in the room, but he knew he would feel her presence nonetheless. Louisa walked down the hallway and stepped forgivingly in front of Lucas, opened the door and walked into the room, then turned on the lights as if to prove to him that the ghosts he feared were not there. It was just a room. An ordinary room filled with the possessions of an ordinary little girl.

"Come in and see for yourself, Lucas," she said.

He took one slow step past the threshold and paused, waiting for the inevitable dread to pass. The dread that people face when they have to see and touch the things of someone lost, then relive every memory that those things carry with them. They are conduits to the past. Sometimes the memories are happy; others are painful. But remembering, and laughing or crying as they pass through you, is the only way to continue on with your life.

He took a deep breath as he moved forward another step, and looked around. Her room was so much smaller than he remembered, and as he looked at the things laid about on the bed and the dresser, and the pictures Eliza had hung on her walls and tacked to the closet door, a feeling settled over him that he hadn't expected; it made him smile.

It wasn't the morbid tomb he'd envisioned. It was a warm, happy place. A room where a sweet young girl had spent hours of joy and solitude, dreaming of wonderful things to come. It was sad that those things would never be, but still, the room held no malice. It was a happy place.

The bed was small and perfectly suited for a little girl, covered with a lavender comforter over the mattress and a frilly laced skirt that hung to the floor.

She had large, fluffy pillows scattered on top, so she could sit on it like a sofa when she wanted to read or play games by herself. The window above the bed looked out through the pines and over the rocky valley, towards the city of Palma.

Her dresser was an antique pine four-drawer that her mother found in a little shop on the French Riviera. She had always loved keeping her clothes neatly folded in the drawers, imagining that someone famous had once owned it and the spirits of their clothes mingled with hers.

On top of the dresser was an oval shaped mirror in a brass swivel frame, and lying in front of it was a sterling silver hair brush with dark brown horsehair bristles. The brush had been a gift from Eliza's grandmother, who grew up in the Pyrenees of northern Spain, and she told her it once belonged to a princess. Lucas picked it up and sat on the edge of the bed. He held it in his lap and ran his fingertips slowly over the stiff bristles, and they raked softly against his coarse, calloused palm. He turned the brush faceup and saw strands of her hair still wound deeply into it, and he gently pulled them, one by one, free of the brush.

He drew them out and lay them across the bed in a cluster. Eight or ten lengths of long, golden fibers, that together, resembled a flowing ray of sunlight. Eliza's hair had always been a reflection of who she was, and who she would become; a ray of sunlight in the lives of everyone around her. He wound the fibers around his fingers into a small loop and tucked it into his shirt pocket.

The guilt seized him again, "It was all my fault, Louisa. Everything that's happened. It's my fault," he said.

"How could anything that happened be your fault, Lucas?" Louisa asked.

"That day, I was teasing Eliza and she came up to the house alone. And then I,…I was standing on the hill, staring at the women on the beach. If I hadn't been standing there for so long, Eliza would still be here, she would still be alive. Mom would still be alive. Maybe even my father would still be alive, and we would all be together. I was standing there staring, and having thoughts about the women on the beach, when I should have been here for Eliza. I could have saved her."

Louisa sat next to him and put her arm around his shoulder. "Listen to me, Lucas. None of this was your fault. If you had come back to the house with Eliza, or arrived any sooner than you did, those men would have probably killed you. The only thing that would have changed, is that both of you would have been lost. It's craziness to carry this around on your shoulders. What you were thinking and feeling that morning are just the normal things that everyone feels at that age. If you can't let go of it, it will ruin you.

You will never be able to love a woman the way you should."

"I've never loved a woman, Louisa. I never will… it's a madness that destroys me. I can't let it take control of me again."

Chapter Ten

PALMA, MALLORCA

The life of a Legionnaire is never peaceful, never quiet, and rarely alone. For more than a decade, Lucas' life was devoted to either training for war, or being completely submersed in the midst of it. Rising before the sun to train with his brothers, and anticipating the next battle, which might be the last for any one of them. Be prepared to kill; and be prepared to die. Always on alert and never alone; this is the way of the Legionnaires.

Lucas was nervous about coming home to Mallorca, because his last memories were dark and terrible; the first battle he had ever fought, and the worst defeat of his life. A defeat that cost him everything. But what he discovered after just a day or two, was that the house felt oddly peaceful. He opened the windows during the day, to breath the fresh sea air, took long walks down the stone pathways to the shore and around the rocky bay, and let the quiet stillness seep into him.

On the third day, the solitude turned to loneliness. Not so much that he wanted to be surrounded by companions, but just to be among the sounds and smells and sensations of life. To remind himself that he was not alone in this world. He thought it might be nice to drive into Palma in the evening, for a drink or two at one of the fine tapas bars, and surround himself with something normal. Something that he hadn't experienced for a very long time.

He walked down the hill in the dark and across the gravel parking area to the Fiat, and it felt like he was walking through a graveyard, and the dead were whispering in his ears. He tried to ignore the hair prickling on the back of his neck. He curled himself into the small Fiat and drove along the tight twisting coastal road to Palma.

The light from his headlamps swayed left against the rocky cliffs, and then vanished into the black void on the right, where the road ceased and a thousand feet of air hung over the sea below. And across the mountainside, he could see the lights from many homes glinting through the forest that he couldn't see during the day. The lights were comforting, and reassured him that he wasn't quite as alone on the island as he felt. The daytime views of nothing but thick pine forests was an illusion.

Palma was quiet this night. Mostly, the local

Mallorcans making their way home from the stores and shops, and some stopping for a drink with friends. There were a few tourists arriving as well, and they were easy to pick out among the residents. Maps in hand, eyes constantly searching for street signs and markers, and intently analyzing the various menus displayed in front of the cafes and restaurants. They walked a short distance, and then stopped to stare at unique old architecture, or touch the stone-carved statues in the plazas.

Lucas parked his car off the main road, along the line of palms that bordered the bay and small sailing boats lined up along the shore, each leaning against the one next to it like a row of fallen dominos. He walked around the La Seu Cathedral that seemed a thousand feet tall with the bell towers lit at night, and made his way into the city center through the Jardi del Bisbe gardens, slowing his normally furious pace to enjoy the overwhelming scent of early summer flowers.

As he came out of the gardens, he entered the Plaça de Cort, at the very heart of the oldest barrio in Palma. A triangular plaza at the junction of three medieval brick streets, surrounded by five-story buildings of stone, cut from the surrounding hills hundreds of years ago. The ground floor was a mix of shops and cafes, and all of the upper levels were apartments and lofts with tall arched windows and tiny terraces encased by decorative wrought-iron balustrades. Old couples walking arm in arm, and young couples laughing, crisscrossed through the plaça, all in their own little world and enjoying the slow pace of life in Mallorca.

Lucas stood in the center next to the little gurgling fountain, and slowly turned to take it all in. This was the place he always had in his mind when he thought about home. The feeling of old Spain lived in this very place. Across the plaça he saw the Café Española; lights burning low inside and a few people, but not too many entering and leaving. It seemed the perfect place to spend an hour or two.

The front door was dark wood with peeling varnish, and a frosted glass window above, and as he stepped inside, it was typically narrow like a long hallway. A mix of tall standing tables, and small round ones with three chairs each, pressed close to the right side of the narrow room. The floor tiles bore the influence of the Moors, with brown and green and yellow designs that resembled opening flower buds; the ceiling was high, and the plaster weathered and cracked, with faint brown water-stains from the leaky roof. The bar was in the very back of the room, and it was completely empty, save for a pretty young girl behind it, cleaning wine glasses.

There were only a few locals inside, standing around the tall tables and nibbling on tapas and drinking wine or sherry. They all stopped, and stared at him warily as he walked to the end of the bar and sat on a stool, but soon they went back to their meals and conversation. He sat for two hours and sipped a fresh seafood bisque and drank a few beers, which instantly labeled him as an outsider, but he was content that no one in the town had recognized him as the boy who'd been suspected of killing his own sister all those years ago.

At 12:30 he paid his tab and walked out into the quiet street and turned east along the Carrer Del Palau. He could smell the salty sea air as the road went straight to the harbor, and could hear work at the marina going on, even at this late hour. Then he heard something else. Something his ears were trained to detect amid all the normal sounds of life in a village or town. A muffled cry.

He stopped dead in his tracks and turned his head to triangulate to the source. There it was again. Further down the hill and to the left.

He moved stealthily now, rolling forward in his sandals from heel to toe. Two steps, then pause and listen. He eased up to the edge of an alley, went down to his knees to get below the normal sightline, and peeked around the corner with only one eye.

He could smell the powerful stench of urine where young British and Dutch tourists had used the alley as a toilet after their evenings in the bars, and the odor of rotting food in trash bins had soaked into the lime-plaster walls. Looking away from the well-lit streets into the alley, his vision was bad at first, but then his eyes adjusted to the darkness and he could see movement. It was a struggle, or a fight. Then he heard the cry again. A girl's plea to stop.

That same dark, empty madness that had seized him in Tipasa, came over him again. He moved gracefully and silently like a cat, staying in the shadows against the wall. As he got closer, he saw two men holding a girl down. In the shadowy darkness, he could only tell that she was young, perhaps in her teens, with long black hair and wearing a schoolgirl dress. One of the men was pinning her to the street with his knees and holding a hand over her mouth; the other working feverishly to bind her feet and arms with a length of rope.

He came in low from the shadows, behind the man trying to tie the girl, slipped his arm around his neck until his elbow tucked neatly into the man's windpipe, and locked it back into a choking V-shaped vise. He squeezed his hold tight in the same instant, and the man's vocal cords went dead. He tried to scream, but nothing came out.

Lucas jerked him upright, then stomped the backside of his right calf, which buckled his legs and drove his kneecap straight into the bricks with a horrible "crunch" like a raw eggshell breaking.

The other lowlife, who was pinning the girl down, was startled by the silent attack, and he jumped up and backpeddled into a group of trash cans, which turned the quiet alley into a cacophony of banging tin cymbals. He took one look at his partner being choked to death, and took off down the alley.

Lucas cinched his chokehold tighter and held it until the struggler went limp and he could feel the full weight of his body hanging in his arms. Then he let the sack of shit fall face-first into the street.

The young girl was still lying there, retreating into a fetal position and sobbing. He reached out his hand gently, "Shh, it's ok now. You're safe."

Her eyes were filled with terror and she started to shake in spasms, and then she looked into Lucas' eyes, and reached out to take his hand. He pulled her up to her feet, and she wrapped herself around him like his body was the only safe place on the island. He let her hold tight, and held her head in his hands, "No one is going to hurt you. I've got you," he said.

A few lights turned on at the end of the alley, and an old man in a tattered robe wandered out onto the stairs to see what had caused the loud racket.

"Señor, please call the police. This girl was attacked and I got one of them," Lucas yelled to him.

The old man looked afraid and shook his head; then disappeared quickly back into the house and turned off the lights.

"He's not going to help, he's afraid," the girl said, as she looked down at the body on the ground. "We need to leave quickly. They'll come back for him, and they'll kill us both when they get here."

"Who will kill us?" Lucas said.

"The men from the sea. The ones who steal girls, and they are never seen again."

Lucas turned and walked towards the street with the young girl clinging to him. His mind was racing backward now, thinking of Eliza.

When they reached the main street, he stopped and pulled loose from the grasp she had around his waist. "Do others know about this?"

"Yes. It happens every year when the big fishing boats arrive from the south. But no one talks about it. Girls vanish, and the police do nothing."

The police. Lucas remembered the endless torment of the local police, and how they refused to believe him. They kept twisting his words and his recollection until it didn't make sense anymore. He knew exactly what he saw. He knew that Eliza was taken in the van by those two men. But the police wouldn't accept it.

"Tell me more about the big fishing boats from the south," Lucas said.

The girl's panic returned. She was looking around to see who else might be watching them in the full light of the main street. "I can't say anything else, it's too dangerous for my family!" Then she pulled away from him and ran down the street.

She stopped for an instant and turned, "Thank you for saving me!" Then she was gone into the night.

. . .

THE MOST COMMON reaction to a tragedy when it happens, is to feel like you are the only person in the world that it's ever happened to. Lucas had never even wondered if any other little girls had been taken from this place, until he found the littlest girl in Tipasa. He was so absorbed by the loss of Eliza, that it wouldn't have occurred to him. So, Eliza wasn't the first, nor the only girl who had ever been abducted from Mallorca. And likely not the last.

Lucas walked back to the harbor and to the car, all the while expecting to hear a police siren, or ambulance racing into the city center, but none ever came. He wondered how often this happened, if it had always been happening and he just never knew about it, living in the sheltered world of wealthy homes along the shore. He drove back to Port d'Andratx, and when he stepped out this time and walked into the open gravel parking lot, he didn't feel like a terrified seventeen-year-old boy. He felt something else. He felt an angry, vengeful rage burning in the pit of his belly.

He wasn't going to leave this island until he'd turned over every rock to see what slimy creatures were hiding underneath.

Chapter Eleven

PUNTA DE MANRESA

L ucas slept late, after not getting to bed until the early morning hours. He woke to the aroma of freshly brewed coffee, and the enchanting sound of steamy biscuits as the lid was being lifted from a cast iron skillet.

"That smells wonderful," he said as he walked into the kitchen.

Louisa turned and smiled, "I thought you might need something warm in your stomach this morning. My husband was up late too, and he saw you driving in last night, from our cabaña down below. Did you have some fun in town?"

"It was an interesting night," he said, but offered no more details.

He poured a cup of coffee into a little ceramic espresso cup, and walked to the large windows in the salon, to look out at the sea. For most of the night, he'd been thinking about what the girl said; the hint about the men from the sea in the fishing boats.

He walked back into the kitchen and reached over Louisa's shoulder to pull a biscuit from the pan. She tapped the back of his hand to scold him, like she had many times when he was a boy doing exactly the same thing. He laughed, and broke it open and drew the warm doughy scent to his nose and closed his eyes. It was one of the best recollections of his childhood, and happier days here in this house.

"I thought I might go buy some fresh sea bass today. But not at the markets; I'd like to get it directly from the fishing boats. Which marina do those boats come into to ice their catch, do you know?" he asked.

"My husband could get that for you today. Why don't you let him do it?"

"I'd really enjoy going for a drive anyway, and I've never been to the fishing marinas. Father would never let me go when I was young. Just tell me how to get there," he said.

"The best marina is on the other side of the island, at Punta de Manresa. But be wary of which boats you go to, because the North African fisherman are coming in this time of year, and they'll cheat you blind on the price of fish."

"North Africans? I'll keep an eye out for them."

LUCAS LEFT AFTER LUNCH, it was only an hour-and-a-half drive to the port of Punta de Manresa; back through Palma and then straight across the island on Ma-13, driving in the shadows of the Sierra de Tramuntana mountains. Punta de Manresa was a large horseshoe-shaped bay with a deep harbor, and most of the fishing boats from Morocco and Algeria tended to cluster close to each other at the far end of the pier.

He arrived as many of the boats were just starting to come in after dragging their nets offshore in the morning. Sitting on a grassy hill above the bay, he watched and counted the boats, making notes in a small journal. He included descriptions of the boats and how well cared-for they appeared.

One of the last to arrive in the port had just the look he expected. Bright blue paint that was chipping and peeling, and rusted from hard use in the sea, and little maintenance. The main net riggings were weak and awkwardly wired together. The engine was tired and billowing twice as much black smoke from the diesel fuel as a well maintained engine. He shifted all of his focus to that one boat.

They docked far away from the rest of the fleet, and three deck hands began unloading bails of fish into drums on the dock. A decent haul, but it seemed less than the other boats; and another worker from one of the warehousing sheds in the port came down with a rolling dolly and moved the drums back to the shed to be iced.

Lucas decided to get a closer look.

He came down the hill and walked along the main harbor road, stopped to appear interested in other boats, and spoke to a few of the other fishermen before arriving at the final dock. He'd been smart, and wore sandals and slacks and a nice shirt that made him stand out as an early season tourist on holiday. The kind of mainlander that might show up at the docks from time to time, wanting to buy a big fish straight from the sea to impress his friends at dinner.

As he sauntered up to the rusty old fishing boat, the deck hands were watching. He heard them speaking in a mixmash of Arabic and French.

In purely Catalan Spanish, he asked, "How's the catch today? I was hoping to buy a sea bass."

They kept working, loading the fish into the drums as if they didn't understand him.

He pointed to the fish, and said again, "Fish. Fish, I want to buy fish!"

One of the deck hands grunted, and pointed up the dock to the shed, without ever looking up at him.

"Gracias!" he answered.

The large tin shed was across the main dock road, and backed up to a vine-covered hillside. As he approached, he could smell the overpowering stench of fish that was several days past prime.

There were barrels stacked in rows inside the shed, and an old ice machine in the front corner. Its feet weren't leveled, and the machine wobbled and clunked as its electric motor worked the evaporator coils.

The man moving the drums of fish from the boat to the shed was standing in the doorway when he walked up. He had sun-darkened skin, and was wearing oil-stained canvas pants and a long, bright yellow rubber apron that hung around his neck. He had the appearance of a Moroccan or Algerian, like the others.

"Fish. Can I buy fish?" Lucas asked, pointing at the drums.

The man answered in French, and shook his head, "Ne pas vender." (No sell)

"But I want to buy a fish!" Lucas said, again in Catalan.

This time, the man responded more threateningly, "Ne pas vender! Partez maintenant!" (Go away now!)

Lucas raised his hands as he surrendered to the threats and backed away in an apologetic retreat. *I'll see you later, shit-head.* He thought to himself.

PERCHED BACK ON THE HILLSIDE, he watched for several more hours, and as the sun was falling below the horizon and the blue water began to shimmer in shades of yellows and red, his calm vigil was shattered.

He heard the engine first. An old Citroën four cylinder, with the valves so worn and dry of oil, the clatter could be heard a mile away. He turned his head to see what was coming down the dock road, and there it was. The old, rusted blue van that had haunted him for years.

He subconsciously drew in a deep breath and held it, then slowly let half the breath out and paused. The subconscious killing rhythm of a sniper. If he'd had a rifle it might have all ended right there. He was fixated on the van as it chunked along the dock road, and then, the doors opened to the same shed being used by the Moroccan fisherman, and it pulled inside. Then the doors were quickly closed behind it.

Chapter Twelve

PUNTA DE MANRESA

❦❦❦

As darkness fell on Mallorca, hell was about to fall on the docks in Punta de Manresa.

Lucas had slowly worked his way down the hillside and into the port, where several dozen vehicles were parked. Most belonged to fisherman, longshoremen, ship builders, and day-laborers. He knew if he broke into enough of them, he'd eventually find a weapon. He scored on the second. An old Mercedes utility van, that was once a creamy white, but now mostly shades of orange and brown from the rust that burst through the paint and dribbled down the sides. In the rear floorboard he found a tool box with a long slender fillet knife; and among the regular tools, a ball-peen hammer designed to drive large steel rivets. He took them both.

He scaled the hill just enough to crawl slowly

through the shrubs and thick vines for cover, and down the side that backed up to the shed. Keeping a careful eye on it, he hadn't seen anyone come or go since the blue van arrived. He thought only the one arrogant Moroccan from earlier was still in the shed, but he didn't know how many others might have arrived with the driver in the van. For sure, there were at least two to deal with.

Slithering out of the green leaves, he melded his body to the wall of the shed; pressed his ear against the tin, and listened. He could hear a few mumbled words. Then the sound of metal lightly screeching like fingernails on a blackboard, as they slid a steel drum across the floor.

The shed had no windows to peer into for reconnaissance, and no side doors for a flanking entry. Like it or not, he'd have to come in blind through the heavy, rolling front door. If he opened it himself, he'd have at least one hand occupied with the door and one left to fight with. If all of the men were at the back of the shed when he rolled the door open, it would give them time to arm themselves. He needed to trick one of them into coming to the front and pulling the door open for him.

SANITY, logic, decency; all of the workings of normal minds went out the window.

Lucas was dead sure of two things. First, that was absolutely the van involved in the abduction of his little sister. And second, anyone connected with that van was going to take their last breath tonight. He didn't give a shit if they weren't there twelve years ago when it happened. He considered it guilt by association, and he was going to kill anyone that smelled even remotely guilty.

He reached down and cinched the straps tight on his sandals so they wouldn't come off during a sprint or a struggle, and then pulled his loose-fitting shirt off over his head. He wanted to make it as difficult as possible to get a hold on him, if it came to a belly-to-belly fight. He had a light sweat building, and as he moved along the front of the shed, the moonlight made his lean, hard body glisten and blend with the galvanized metal siding behind him.

He eased up to the front and positioned himself on the opposite side of the rolling door, so that whoever opened it would be looking straight out at the bay, while he came at them from the side.

He reached over and banged twice on the metal, and spoke lightly in French with an Arabic accent, "Eh, open the door."

It was silent for a moment, and then a voice yelled back, "Achmed, is that you?"

"Oui," Lucas softly responded.

He heard a chain clatter as it was pulled through a hasp on the other side of the door, and then the rusty rollers on the bottom of the door squealed as it began to roll open. The man who stepped out into the dark was the same one from this morning. As he took a step forward, the hammer was already in full swing to center mass.

The peen-shaped end struck him just at the tip of his sternum with the force of a freight train, snapping his head forward as his trunk caved in. His heels stayed planted and his body went backward and hit the floor with a thud, and his arms went straight up and stiffened as if he were reaching for some unseen object in the air.

The force of the blow not only fractured his chest bone, but demolished the soft tissue of the heart below it. Shit-head number one, was done.

As he came in the open doorway there was a guy jumping out of the back of the van, and he grabbed a piece of pipe laying on top of a drum and came running straight at Lucas.

Lucas drew the hammer back in a full arm swing and threw it spinning across the shop at the attacker, but it sailed high and smashed into the wall of the shed with a "bang" that was deafening. Even though it missed its mark, the hammer whizzing over his head made the guy stop in his tracks for just a second, and that was all Lucas needed to cover the distance.

He caught the swinging pipe in his left hand as he arrived and slashed the fillet knife across the man's throat with his right, in one smooth motion. The guy grabbed his neck for an instant, and then folded to the floor as the blood stopped flowing to his brain.

Lucas quickly scanned left, looking for any movement, or structures that might hide an attacker, then pivoted back to his right towards the van. And then he saw him. Stepping slowly out from in front of the van. A dark figure in the shadows; a dark-skinned man. That same dark-skinned, mono-browed bastard who took Eliza twelve years ago!

Lucas had been focused, almost stoic in his assault up to this point. But now his emotions came flooding up into his chest. This was the moment of vengeance he'd seen in his dreams, and now he was strong enough, and brave enough to carry it out.

The dark man came slowly out into the light, and just as he had all those years ago, he reached behind and drew a long, rusty blade from his belt. He glanced down at his companion bleeding out on the floor, and then back up at Lucas. No sign of concern or care. He came forward now, slowly sliding his front foot ahead, and then drawing his rear to catch up, keeping his balance centered all the while.

Lucas had seen this before. Whoever he was, he'd been trained to kill with a knife, and he knew what he was doing. Lucas had trained with one, but never needed anything more than firearms in combat to get the job done. As the Specs Ops guys always said, "Shit has to fall really bad to get down to fighting with just a knife," so they rarely trained with it.

Lucas circled to his right with the slender, fish skinning blade out in front of him. The dark man paused, and let him move. He was baiting him. Then just as Lucas took another step, while he had one foot in the air and all of his weight on the other, the dark man lurched forward. He looked like he was coming high, but at the last second he dove low and swiped the long blade across Lucas' inner thigh. He was targeting his femoral artery. Going for the leg-kill. But the cut was shallow and to the outside. It stung like hell, but it wasn't fatal.

Lucas winced and gritted his teeth and jumped back two steps. He couldn't make any mistakes with this guy or he was going to end up dead.

Eliza would never forgive me for that. He thought to himself.

He moved to the right again. One big step. Then another. He was watching the dark man's eyes as they followed his feet, and plotted his next attack. He could see it in his eyes; Mono-Brow was a one-trick pony. He favored the leg attack and nothing else. So Lucas stepped again, offering him his sweetest move.

In the middle of the third step he came again, but Lucas was waiting for it. He thrust his left hand down and blocked the knife, then swung back around and hacked through the man's knife hand, completely severing two of his fingers. The long rusty blade clattered to the floor, and two digits tumbled and rolled next to it. The dark man wasn't silent now, he howled like a wounded banshee.

Lucas quickly followed up by grabbing him by the hair and yanking his head down, and at the same time driving his knee up into the dark man's face. It knocked him into a stupor and sent him to the floor. Lucas was sitting on his chest in a flash, with the point of the slender blade piercing his throat.

As he drove the sharp edge deep, he saw his eyes glaze, and when the wheezing last breath came from his lungs, a light steamy mist followed it up into the air. He watched with a calm fascination, and suddenly had a flashback to his first kill; high on the mountainside in the Central African Republic.

HE COULD SEE his sergeant's face smiling as they slipped quietly away from the hide where he'd made the shot that killed the African warlord, and then he turned and said, "*The soul of every evil bastard you kill in this world, will be your servant in the next life.*"

Lucas looked at the bodies scattered around the floor of the shed, and whispered, "Three souls for you, Eliza."

AS HE STOOD up over the dark man's body, Lucas looked up at the van with both of the back doors spread open. He saw things that didn't belong.

Sandals and small shoes; a little brown purse and a pink sweater. Things that belonged to little girls, that the men hadn't yet gathered and thrown away. He recorded it into his mind, made a quick search of the shed for other evidence, then moved quickly to leave the bloody scene.

Chapter Thirteen

THE VILLA

Lucas peered around the edge of the rolling doorway and out into the moonlit harbor. He suddenly felt trapped like a rat in a can. The battle had been over in minutes, but it wasn't exactly silent and he knew there were more men in this crew of jackals that were out there somewhere. If they were aboard the fishing boat they might have been too far away to hear the banging metal and death howls coming from the shed, but if they heard it they'd likely be coming prepared for a fight. He would lose his only advantage: surprise.

His senses were still amplified from the surge of adrenaline and he could see farther and sharper into the nightscape. The tall net booms on the sea vessels tied to the long dock tipped left and right in a rolling rhythm from the wind-driven waves. The sea beyond was a silvery backdrop, and even though it was a cloudless night, the sky was black and the stars muted by the moon.

He could smell the salt so heavy in the air that it seared his nostrils, and as he opened his mouth to breathe deeply he could taste the acrid odor of rotting fish in the back of his throat. Every part of him was flush with hormonal stimulants, even his skin was blistering with goosebumps and the light breeze felt like sandpaper scratching across the surface.

When he was sure it was clear, he slipped around the door and slid along the outer wall and back the way he came in; up into the scrubby brush along the hillside behind the sheds and through the tree line above, until he reached the pathway that led to the street where he had parked his car, a mile from the harbor. He doubled back along his trail twice to make sure he wasn't being followed, and on the third pass went directly to the car and drove away quickly.

He stayed on the country lanes that wound through the hills away from Palma, and on sections that were well lit by the moon, he turned off his headlights and drove in darkness, pulling off the road occasionally to watch and listen. He had followed the same pattern many times in the past years. After making a shot from a high cliff face or a thickly forested hill, he was trained to egress in a way that defied pattern recognition and predictability, and frequently check his backtrail. He killed from afar, and then slipped silently away.

But this killing was different. This killing wasn't calculated and planned, or executed with cold precision from a hide, far from the intended victim. It wasn't as mechanical as aligning a precision made weapon from a safe place, isolated from emotions. A vacuum of space where the assassin calms his beating heart and synchronizes his trigger release to the rhythm.

No, this killing was very different. It was spontaneous, and fueled with rage. It was passionate, and chaotic. It was an intimate taking of human life; gazing into their eyes as he bartered for possession of their souls. Never in his life had Lucas experienced anything like the murder of these three men.

BY THE TIME he drove into the gravel parking area below the villa, the adrenaline had seeped away and he could feel the sharp burning sensation from sliced flesh on his thigh, opened to the stinging salty air. He came up the hill and into the villa; Louisa had left on the outdoor lights along the walk and the lights in the kitchen and salon were turned low.

His leg was beginning to stiffen and ache, and he went directly into the kitchen and opened the pantry door where Louisa had always stored exactly what he needed to treat the knife wound. He rummaged through the bottles and jars until he found it; a jar of honey, imported from the lavender fields of Andalusia. He dipped two large spoonfuls of the golden gooey syrup into a pan, and turned it on to boil.

He found a small sewing kit in his mother's top drawer, brought it back into the kitchen and sat at the table. When the honey was hot, he took a wooden spoon and worked it deep into the incision made by the rusty knife blade. It wouldn't have been a bad idea to get a tetanus shot, but in this case it might bring unwanted attention from the police.

The Legionnaires all learned emergency battlefield first aid, and honey was known to have natural anti-infection properties, while raw sugar was often used to heal and close a wound. The hot honey burned like a bastard, but he gritted his teeth and smeared it in, then closed the wound with a needle and thread and eighteen tight stitches.

The sharp pain from treating the knife wound cleared his head. He started thinking about what he'd seen in the old blue van in the shed, and the magnitude of it all settled into his mind.

"This isn't a few thugs stealing young girls for their own pleasure. This is business. A well-orchestrated abduction and smuggling operation; just like Tipasa. They are slave traders," he said out loud. "No way those three toads at the shed were smart enough to plan and operate this, or pay for it. Who's really at the center of all this?"

Then something else came to his mind. It seemed like they were targeting young local girls in the inner city or small towns. Girls whose disappearance wouldn't demand the kind of media attention as Eliza's did those years ago. Was she a mistake?

His gut told him no. She'd been targeted.

Chapter Fourteen

ALGIERS

Agold-plated cellular telephone lying atop a mahogany night stand, rang with a delicate sound like angel bells in a church. On the third ring, a man picked it up, inspected the caller I.D., and pressed the green button.

"What news do you have?"

"Your Excellency, three more men have been murdered. They were all lower level operatives from the fishing crew, and easily replaced. But the location of our operation in Mallorca may have been compromised," the caller said.

The man holding the golden phone gazed out the porthole of the forward suite on the yacht. He watched the blue water pass by as the nearly two-hundred foot vessel sailed in a northeasterly heading against the prevailing winds and a three-foot rolling sea. "The gathering is scheduled in Palma for one week from today. Is there any need to abort our plans?"

"I don't believe that's necessary, Your Excellency."

"Is this loss in any way connected to the man we lost in Tipasa a short time ago? And more importantly, could they all be related in some way to the Spaniard?"

"That is yet to be determined. However, I will find the answer; I swear it."

"Find out who is responsible, and kill them. Quickly."

"Yes, Your Excellency."

Chapter Fifteen

BARCELONA, SPAIN

Lucas was sitting out on the stone terrace in a reclining deckchair, laid back nearly horizontal as he gazed up at the stars, and nursing his pain with an expensive French cognac he found in the cellar. He had turned off all the lights in the house to make it as dark as possible on the terrace. The moon was trailing late now, and the night was so black he could even see the stars that normally hid from view and the dark voids where none seemed to exist. He was lightly rolling the lock of yellow hair twisted in a ring around his fingers, and thinking of her.

He had finally avenged her. It didn't seem possible after all these years had passed, that he would randomly stumble into the same men who had taken Eliza, but somehow it happened. For the last twelve years he'd dreamed of killing the dark man, and he always envisioned it as the moment that would liberate him from his guilt. But he didn't feel liberated at all. In fact, he felt like he was just getting started; that there were a lot more out there somewhere who needed to be found and dealt with.

He stood and stretched his bandaged leg, looked back into the terrace window and saw his own reflection in the darkened glass, staring back. Everything was different now. The world he thought he knew; the man he thought he was; and what he thought he might do with his life beyond the Legion. It was all about to change.

Then a random thought popped into his head, "What if I could kill them all…"

THE TELEPHONE in the salon began to ring. He glanced down at his Luminox Evo military watch; the glowing hands showed 2:00 a.m. "Who would be calling at this hour? And who would even know that I was here?" he thought. As he reached the open french doors the ringing stopped. He paused and wondered if it might have been just a misdialed number. Then it began to ring again.

He picked up the telephone receiver, and held it to his ear but didn't speak.

"Hello, Lucas. It seems you've developed a habit

of rescuing young girls and killing bad men," Diggs said.

"How did you get this number?" Lucas answered.

Diggs answered, "That's an unimportant detail, Lucas. You have more important things to be concerned about. Can you guess what those things might be?"

Lucas held the phone against his chest and stared out into the night sky and thought for a moment, then brought it back to his ear, "If you know about the men I killed yesterday, then someone else probably knows about it."

Diggs answered in a deep, slow whisper, "Yes." Then he added, "It was quite curious that you came across the same team that took your sister, and more curious still that you survived it. Maybe it was fate."

"How in the hell do you know all of this? Are you watching me?" Lucas said.

"We've been watching you for a long time, Lucas. Waiting to see if you might be up to the task."

"Task? What task?"

"Again, that's not an important detail at the moment. Stay focused. You've stirred up a real shit storm, and the truly dangerous men are on their way to Mallorca as we speak. I can't say whether or not they know who killed their snatch team on the docks, but sooner or later they'll put it all together. The next flight off that rock is at 5:25, Iberia flight 1080 to

Barcelona. There's a ticket waiting for you at the check-in desk. Don't miss that flight."

Lucas' mind was swirling now. He was neck deep in murder, and now a man he hardly knew was calling to tell him others were coming to kill him. And, he knew more about Lucas than he let on when they met in Algeria. He also knew about Eliza's kidnappers.

"How much do you know about my sister? And who's watching me?" Lucas said.

"Try to put that out of your mind for now. Once you arrive in Barcelona, find a discreet method of transportation and go to Monte Carlo. I know you have business to attend to there. You'll need to travel with cash; don't use any credit cards. Do you have cash?"

"A few hundred euros, that's it," Lucas said.

"We can solve that. Do you still remember how to open your father's safe in the house in Barcelona?"

"Yes, I'll always remember that combination."

Lucas' father hadn't been overly clever with the safe combination, using the birthdays of Lucas, Eliza, and his mother; but he rarely kept anything more than personal documents and a small amount of cash in it. He thought it was best to keep it simple, in case someone else in the family needed access to it when he wasn't around. Turned out he was right.

"Good. There will be a sizable sum waiting for you in the safe, and the spare key is where it always was in the garden. Take the money and buy a vehicle that won't stand out. You'll understand everything in time; but for now, get to Monte Carlo and follow the scent of money."

Then Diggs added, "And one more thing, Lucas; the killing isn't over. It's just beginning."

"Wait, how do you…," before Lucas could speak, the phone clicked and changed into a droning dial tone.

LUCAS GATHERED a few clothes into his duffel, left a note for Louisa on the front door telling her to stay away from the house until he returned, and left for the airport.

AT 6:47 in the morning, Lucas walked down the jetway at El Prat International Airport in Barcelona. He took his time before collecting his duffel, and bought a lukewarm croissant with prosciutto and cheese in the food court, before stepping out into the humid morning air. He loved Barcelona as a boy, but he wasn't in any hurry to return to the house that had felt like a solitary tomb during the last year he lived here alone.

The universally identifiable black-and-yellow taxis were lined up in orderly fashion just outside the baggage claim, and he took the first. As they drove into the city on Avinguda de la Granvia, the thing that he'd forgotten about Barcelona, the thing he had always loved the most, came rushing back to him; the colors. Barcelona was a city of spectacular, vibrant, glowing color.

Everywhere he looked, the buildings were tiled or painted in the most exquisite greens and blues and reds, yellows and orange and bright purple. There were buildings like those you'd see in children's make-believe story books, with flowing shapes and hand-drawn windows, and tall spires that reached to the sky; all of them alive with the colors of the rainbow.

Lucas smiled, then laughed out loud, spinning his head in all directions as they drove through the cultural center and into the barrios.

Then the taxi slowed and pulled to the curb.

"This is the house, Señor," the driver said.

Lucas looked out the side window, but didn't immediately open the door. Like a convict hoping that he might be able to stay on the bus and be forgotten, rather than stepping out and walking through the prison gates; Lucas wasn't in a hurry to go inside.

"Can you wait for me? I'll just be a minute, and I'll leave my bag here," he said.

He stepped out of the taxi, took a deep breath, and walked deliberately to the front step. He found the rock that hid the spare key, in the flower bed, and opened the door. He rushed in like he was making an entry into a hostile environment. If he'd had a gun, it would have been drawn and sweeping in front of him, ready to take out the first moving target.

The door to his father's study was unlocked, and he was relieved that he didn't have to kick it open in his hurry to get out of there. He pulled up the carpet that covered the floor safe, and quickly spun the dial.

Inside, he found two giant stacks of euros, wrapped with freshly glued seals; at least one-hundred thousand. "Whew, Diggs wasn't kidding." He stuffed one into each of his front pockets, and left as quickly as he came.

He jumped into the back of the taxi, "I need to buy a reliable used car; know of a dealer that won't rob me?"

"Si, Señor. I have a cousin who sells cars!" said the driver.

"Help me get a good deal, and I'll give you a hundred euro tip for the ride."

As the taxi pulled away from the curb, Lucas took one last look at the huge brick house and felt a pang of sadness. He hated, after so many good years and happy memories in the home, that he detested it so badly now. It belonged to him now that his father was gone, but he would never step foot in it again if he could help it.

Forty minutes later, as they were passing the barrio

Montegala, and beginning to see scattered automobile dealers along the avenue, Lucas spotted something that caught his attention. He sat up in the seat and tapped the driver on the shoulder, "Stop here, I saw what I want in that lot we just passed."

"But my cousin, Diego, has many fine cars, Señor!"

"I'll still give you the hundred euro tip if I buy what I saw. Just turn around!"

Chapter Sixteen

CÉRET, SOUTH OF FRANCE

I t was a rash and impulsive thing to do. The kind of thing a very young man with wild dreams and cash in his pocket, would do. Lucas had skipped completely over that stage of life when he decided to join the Foreign Legion, or maybe that was actually all of his inevitable impulses thrown in one grand roll of the dice. But now his life in the Legion was over, and even though he was old enough to know better, it seemed he was still too young to resist.

He walked slowly around her, reaching out a few times to touch the glimmering paint. It was freshly waxed and felt like slippery wet glass under his fingertips. She had sensuous lines and curves; a narrow waist and firm saddle. He knelt down to admire the mechanical muscle nestled in her underbelly.

A twelve-hundred cc, Boxer engine that generates

more raw horsepower than most mid-sized automobiles, wedged into a light tubular steel frame. And two polished aluminum wheels, wrapped in Michelin rubber, to send all that power to the pavement.

Unlike the modern Italian racers that flashed along the Riviera, the BMW 1200 RS was a mix of the old world and the new. A battle-tested motorcycle design that was both hardened and refined for ultimate reliability, and fast as hell.

He was planning on traveling light and fast, entering Monaco by land in a less conspicuous way than by airplane. If anyone was on his trail and looking for him, the airport would be a death trap, and on the twisting mountainous two-lanes of southern France and Monaco, the motorcycle would be uncatchable.

He rode north out of Barcelona on the E-15 freeway, and then switched to the AP-7 towards Girona. He peeled around the city and took the endless switchbacks through the Catalonian mountains, getting acquainted with the big BMW as she heeled over on her side through the curves and roared down the straightaways. He exited Spain and crossed into France on an unmarked tarmac road north of Figueres, and made a detour to the hamlet town of Céret.

As he approached, he selected an address that he preloaded into the BMW's GPS, and began to follow the bright red arrow down a country lane, until the road came to an end in front of a small, dilapidated cottage. It was probably stone, but the vines and plants had enveloped the walls to the point of being unable to know for sure.

The tile roof was blackened with mold and had clusters of green moss growing from the cracks and joints, and the front porch hung in a sloping fault to the left. The garden around the cottage had long since been buried by weeds, and invasive plants that stood knee high. It was late in the day and the light was fading, making the old house and surrounding woods feel like an old silver-tone photograph; shades of grey and a grainy texture to the naked eye.

He shut off the drumming engine and listened, but heard nothing stirring around the house. Then he reached up and unbuckled his chin strap and pulled the snug helmet over his head. He heard a creak at the front door and saw a sliver of faint lamplight coming from the opening, then the unmistakable outline of a shotgun barrel sliding through.

"Don't shoot me, Serge. I might be the only friend you'll ever have," Lucas said.

The door opened a bit wider and a head full of tangled hair peeked out to stare into the falling daylight.

"Lucas? Is that you?"

"Of course it's me. Who else would ever come to visit you in this shit hole?"

"Lucas Martell! I can't believe you actually came! How did you make it out of the Legion alive? I thought sure you'd be a maggot bucket in some sandbox in Africa by now," Serge yelled.

"Not hardly."

"You aren't here on Legion business are you?" the little Frenchman asked.

"You're safe from the Legion, Serge; they want nothing more to do with you. I've got some business in Monaco. The kind of business that you're uniquely qualified to help me with. I need to requisition some hardware," Lucas said.

"Pull your bike around back where it won't be seen, and come on in. Let's crack open a bottle and you can tell me what you need."

LUCAS PUSHED the big bike around the house and parked her behind a tool shed, then covered her with a canvas tarp. Inside the house, Serge set up two marginally clean glasses and poured a round of Amorik whiskey. Serge was a native Frenchman who joined the Foreign Legion at the same time as Lucas. He was about the same age, and similarly had virtually no friends or family. He enlisted in hopes of finding a purpose for his life.

He was short and thin, with wiry ginger colored hair, wide ears and distinctively large teeth, which earned him the call-name, "Rat" in the squad. Lucas and Serge bonded almost instantly, being outcasts with a slight death wish. He'd been by Lucas' side for nearly eight years in the Legion, and was known as the best armorer in the African theater.

He had a way with guns. He loved them, cared for them, spoke to them secretly when no one was watching, and nothing he worked on ever failed to function in life-or-death combat. When he tuned a rifle, it shot true to any distance desired, and a miss could always be faulted to the shooter, not the rifle.

He also had an unmanageable temper, and went into fits of rage that frequently sent him to the stockade and ultimately, out of the Legion. It was in defense of his best friend that he finally crossed the line a bit too far. One night, as the squad had taken leave and were exploring the back streets of the capital city, Bangui, in search of professional female company, an argument arose.

A few of the Legionnaires in the team began to question why Lucas never joined them in their forays to the brothels, and then one particularly stupid German, who was new to the squad, used the word, "Poof." The ensuing riot brought out most of the local police force, and the German never fully recovered from the beating he received at the hands of "Rat." Serge spent six months in a military prison in central France, then was dishonorably discharged.

Lucas came into the cottage and sat at the table across from Serge, and smiled as he raised the glass of whiskey, "Santé!" he said, and they both emptied the glasses into their mouths.

"Tell me what you need, Lucas," Serge said with an anxious stare. He was excited to have his skills needed again.

"I'm going to Monte Carlo, so it needs to be discreet. Portable, concealable; something for close range with a lot of punch, but quiet, so it will need a suppressor."

Serge nodded his head in silent consideration, then poured another finger of whiskey into each glass. He hadn't had a visitor in a very long time, and Lucas was likely the best friend he'd ever had. He wanted to drag this moment out for a while.

"A pistol for close work is easy, I've got something here you'll really like." He walked over to the dirty old sofa in the main part of the cottage and slid one end away from the wall, then pulled up two boards from the flooring to expose a compartment below. He reached into the dark hole and pulled up a small plastic case, and then put it on the table in front of Lucas.

He sat back down across from him, and wriggled in his chair with a broad smile, like a kid anxiously waiting for his mother to open a special gift he'd bought with his own money.

"I milled every surface myself, and made the silencer on the lathe in my workshop!" he said.

Lucas opened the case, and tucked neatly into a

fitted foam lining was a Heckler & Koch USP compact pistol. German craftsmanship at it's finest. It had two spare magazines and a short, thick sound suppressor nestled in the foam below the pistol. He pulled the pistol out of the case, held it in his right hand and pushed it forward at eye level, reaching up with his left hand at the same instant in a smooth motion and racking the slide backward. The action of the gun moved like silk.

Serge hopped up and down in his chair and clapped his hands, "Smooth, isn't she?! I worked for days on the slide rails to make them perfect," he said.

Lucas interrupted his joy, "The only thing I'm not sure about is the caliber. This is a .45, Serge; it will only hold ten rounds of ammunition, and it's a very old caliber."

"You only need to shoot a man once with a .45 to put him on the ground, Lucas; not three times like you did with a 9mm. And besides, I built this gun in .45 for the exact reason you need it; silence. A .45 shoots a much larger and heavier bullet at much slower speeds. It didn't take much work to load up special cartridges that have a muzzle velocity below the sound barrier, but they can still punch through a car windshield or a door, and have enough energy to ruin a man's day. With a fat little suppressor, there's no *bang* at all. The only sound you'll hear this gun make is the slide ejecting and chambering another cartridge.

You can fire this over the head of a sleeping baby and not wake him up!"

The sleeping baby analogy was disturbing, but Lucas didn't want to spoil the moment for Serge. The pistol was a little heavier than he was looking for, but he could see the beauty of a weapon that fired with brutal force in near silence.

"I'll take it."

"What about a rifle?" Serge asked.

"I'm just going to see a lawyer and a banker, not making an assault on a warlord."

"Lawyers and bankers are deadly. What about backup, could you use some company?"

"For the moment, I think I can handle the suits without any help."

"Well, can you at least stay a few days? I'd really like the company," Serge said.

"I can't stay more than a day, because there might be people looking for me soon. It could get dangerous around here if they catch up to me, and I don't want to get you killed too."

"What did you do?" Serge asked.

"I left a pile bodies in Mallorca; a few North Africans."

"Did it have anything to do with your sister, Eliza?" he asked. Serge was the only person Lucas had ever spoken to about his sister, and the events that changed his life and drove him to join the Foreign Legion.

After three years serving together, and a long depressing night drinking homemade orange liquor, he shared the story of the worst day of his life. He had shown Serge a small photograph of Eliza that he carried with him, taken on her last day at school in Barcelona. She looked happy in the photo, and it comforted him to think of her happy.

"Yes. I got them, Serge. The men who took her, I killed them. But it turns out they weren't the only snakes in the garden. This thing was bigger than just a few dirtbags, and if I find anyone else who was in on it, I'll put them in the ground too," Lucas said. He sat with his hands wrapped around the empty glass in front of him. Serge reached across the table and poured another sip of whiskey into his friend's glass. He started to speak, but retreated to an understanding silence.

THAT NIGHT, Lucas lay on the crusty old red velvet covered sofa, and looked up through the leaded glass window to see the stars crawling overhead. Sleep came slowly, as Eliza's soft voice constantly whispered in his ear. He could feel her with him, all around him, but suddenly he couldn't remember her face in the same detail as he once could.

The guilt of forgetting stabbed him in the heart, and he rolled on his side to pull his wallet from his trousers. He slipped a finger behind the plastic cover that held his military I.D., and dragged the photo from behind it just far enough to see Eliza's face; stopping before the person to her right in the photo became visible.

At daybreak he woke to a faint, muffled tapping sound; like the light, happy thump of a dog's tail against a hardwood floor. He stretched his arms above his head and arched his back and groaned as his back tightened and ached from the unfamiliar strain of riding a fast motorcycle. He looked around the dusty, dark room but didn't see anything that might have made the noise. He stood and stretched again, then walked out into the morning light on the front porch, and breathed the cool French air.

Then he heard the noise again, a barely perceptible "whup, whup, whup." *What the hell is that?* He thought. He walked around the house along the moss-covered stone path to the workshop, but before he opened the door, he heard Serge's unmistakable laugh up the hill behind the shop.

"What are you up to?" he said as he walked up into the trees.

Serge was sitting at a wooden bench in a clearing, with a unique rifle propped in front of him on a folding bi-pod, pointed into the dense tree line. It was a very secluded shooting range, with a slender line cut through the trees and branches to a target on the next hill, four hundred meters distant. He looked up and smiled as Lucas approached.

"Meet my new sweetheart. Sit here, and let me introduce you," he said.

Lucas took the seat at the bench, and gazed at Serge's masterpiece. It looked more like a dusky black rapier than a rifle. A triangular skeleton stock that folded and locked in place, or could fold forward for travel. The receiver of the gun was lightweight black alloy, with a bolt action and bottom loading magazine, and a large scope mounted to the top with quick disconnect mounts. The barrel was short, with an extended suppressor.

"It's a Nemesis receiver in .338 Lapua Magnum caliber. I know it's a little unusual, but so am I. I machined the barrels myself, with a special twist, and crowned the ends for accuracy. It comes apart in less than 30 seconds, and will fit into a small daypack. Could you hear anything from the house?" Serge asked, raising his eyebrows in an expectant smile.

"Only a muffled thump. I really didn't know what it was, but I wouldn't have guessed it was rifle fire," Lucas said. "But how does it shoot?"

"Look downrange through the scope and tell me what you think."

Lucas slid his eye behind the scope, and the target came into view. A black paper sheet with a one-inch fluorescent dot in the center; and within the dot, a single ragged hole.

"Well you hit the zero at least once, but I heard you shoot several times!" he said.

"That's five rounds, stacked in a single hole, buddy. I zeroed it in at four hundred, but it's accurate out to a mile," he said. "Sure you don't need a long range companion?"

"If the need arises, you'll be the first one I call."

Chapter Seventeen

CAP-D'AIL, FRENCH RIVIERA

ucas rode in along the French Riviera, through the town of Beaulieu-sur-Mer and took the M6098, known as the Princess Grace Highway, twisting through the jagged mountains and cliffs that towered over the coastline and the deep, blue water bay.

He had one stop to make before Monte Carlo; a visit to the local constable's office in Cap-d'Ail. His father's attorney, Jean-Paul Charpentier, had handled all of the details of his cremation, and he was keeping the ashes for Lucas' arrival. But Lucas wanted to see the place where his father died. He couldn't quite explain why, but he needed to see it for himself.

Three kilometers outside of the village, he pulled off the road and into the gravel drive of the small house that was supplied to the constable, as part of his compensation for serving the community. It was a weathered stone cottage from the eighteen century, with white plaster that had patina'd into a rusty orange color that nearly matched the clay tile roof. Here and there, modern brick and mortar patches filled the gaps and cracks that developed over time, and concrete blocks had been quoined into the corners for strength.

He pulled up in front of the walkway and turned off the engine of the BMW, then with the heel of his left boot, clicked out the stand and leaned it over to the left until it was balanced. He swung his right leg over and stood tall and stretched his back; it had been a long ride from Céret with only one brief stop for gas.

The front door of the cottage opened and a short, round little man with wire-rimmed spectacles stepped out onto the landing and stiffened himself up to appear taller. He had sandy colored hair that was thin and wispy on top, he wore gray corduroy pants that were rolled at the bottom to accommodate his short legs, and a black shirt with pearled buttons and a small silver constable's badge. He lifted his chin and inspected Lucas in a very official way, then made sure to announce himself and declare his authority before anything else.

"I am Constable Clément Douven of Cap-d'Ail, may I ask who you are and why you are here?"

Lucas pulled the helmet from his head and hung it lightly over the end of the handlebars on the motorcycle, and stared back in silence for a brief moment before answering. His gaze unnerved the little constable.

"Hello Constable, I am Lucas Martell. I understand that you are the man who found and recovered my father's body from a car crash here a few weeks ago. I'd like a moment of your time," Lucas said.

"Oh, Monsieur Martell! I … I am so sorry for your loss, Monsieur. I will be happy to assist you in any way."

"Thank you, Constable. Would you show me where my father died?"

The constable shuffled his feet awkwardly, and started to twist his hands over as if they were suddenly drenched in sweat. "I could take you there, Monsieur, certainly, but are you sure that is something you wish to see? A scene like that would be very unsettling for most people, and I wouldn't want to bring you any more sadness beyond what you must already be dealing with," the little round man said.

In truth, he found it very difficult to go past that stretch of road himself now, as it disturbed him greatly to have to deal with the fatal car crash. It had been a gruesome spectacle. A dead body hung in the rocks of the steep cliffside, and a smoldering wreckage that had to be winched out with a crane. And the sight and smell of the corpse as it was being removed from the smashed ball of steel that once was an elegant Mercedes sedan, had caused Clément to become so unsettled that he scurried to the closest bushes and vomited until there was nothing left to come up.

He was just a local constable after all, and his normal job was filing reports about stray dogs, or perhaps arbitrating a peaceful solution between quarreling old women, who each disapproved of the other's garden. Dealing with corpses and violent deaths were not things a village constable on the French Riviera normally encountered.

"Constable, I've been a Legionnaire for the past twelve years. I've seen my share of death. The truth is, my father and I parted company on difficult terms. I will never be able to speak to him again, nor to reconcile what happened between us. I feel like I owe it to him to at least go to the place where his life ended and say a prayer for his soul."

The constable smiled weakly, and nodded obediently. Knowing that he was in the presence of a Legionnaire, revered by the French, inspired him to demonstrate his own bravado and return to the scene that had given him nightmares.

Lucas squeezed into the tight passenger seat of the constable's 1974 Citroën CV2, his knees folded tightly against his stomach and his head bent slightly forward against the roof lining. The constable felt a certain pride welling inside him as he started the little French automobile and pulled away, and he rolled the window down and drove slowly through the village so he could smile at all of the local residents, as they went to the steep switchback road where the crash had happened.

The tragedy was still a topic of regular conversation among the locals, and Clément was now anticipating his future tales in the local restaurant of his newest acquaintance, a famed Legionnaire. Hence his slow journey, to make sure everyone saw him with the tall tanned stranger riding in his car.

The constable pointed out the cottage of the old woman who had witnessed the accident, as they passed it, and then as the road began a tight, serpentine twist back and forth down the cliff, he pointed to the missing section of old stone wall along the drop-off, "That is where the car lost control and went through the wall, and then tumbled down to the bottom, Monsieur Martell."

"Please pull over, I'd like to see for myself," Lucas said.

"Certainly."

Lucas pushed open the squeaky door of the Citroën with his right knee and then unfolded himself out of the car. He stood in the middle of the narrow road, looking first back uphill, then down. He knelt down to the road surface, and inspected the asphalt. It had been poured perfectly in the raw, porous way that offered better grip to tires, and rounded for the rain to run off quickly. It was perfectly clean and free of any loose stones or grit, and not a speck of trash or litter.

"The roads here are impeccable, Constable."

The little man smiled, "We take great pride in our community, Monsieur. And our village and the roads are a reflection of that!" he said proudly.

There was something else that Lucas noticed was conspicuously absent, but he didn't mention it to the constable. Any sign of a vehicle losing control on the roadway from excessive speed. There should have been some sign of rubber scorched into the pavement as the car lost traction and the driver attempted to regain control. There was none.

The only marks he did find seemed to indicate something completely different. At the inside edge of the turn, there was a pair of tracks that appeared as though a car backed up into the bushes for a direct run at the wall, as if someone intentionally launched the car straight through the turn and the wall, and over the cliff.

Lucas walked to the edge of the road where the smashed wall was now guarded by a flimsy wire barrier and brightly colored warning tape. He leaned over and looked down at the landscape, nearly vertical with rough and rocky ledges, and outcroppings of grass and thorny shrubs.

He could see the scars in the earth from the first impact, and then a second strike against the rocks thirty feet further down, followed by the gouges of a tumbling steel ball to the bottom. Then a patch of grass blackened and burned where it found its final resting place.

The constable walked slowly up beside Lucas, leaned forward to look over, and then the dizzying height seized him and he snapped backward. He reached up with his right hand and touched his left shoulder, then his right, and then to his forehead and down to finish the sign of the cross as he whispered a blessing.

Chapter Eighteen

MONACO

Maître Jean-Paul Charpentier had served as Francisco Martell's personal lawyer in Monte Carlo for many years. On his recommendation ten years ago, he worked with Francisco to draft a Last Will and Testament which covered his known assets at the time. As is customary under European law, all assets of a deceased husband and father are evenly divided among his survivors; his wife and his children, although in this case Lucas was the only known living heir.

Francisco had mentioned once to his lawyer, that he had received a letter from his son, postmarked from a Legion outpost in the Sudan, and so contacting the French Foreign Legion became his best, and only option for locating Lucas. He didn't even know for certain that Lucas was still alive himself, at the time of Francisco's death.

It was only when Lucas had returned from his assignment in Tipasa with the Fairhope Group, and he contemplated his reenlistment for a fourth term in the Legion, that the message about his father found him. Lucas made his decision quickly; it was time to return to the world. Exactly what world awaited him, he did not know.

The news about his father's death never penetrated beyond the surface of his emotions. He hadn't seen or heard from Francisco in over twelve years, and the two times he wrote letters there had been no response. He assumed that his father still despised him and blamed him for Eliza's kidnapping.

The only mechanism he had for dealing with it, was to completely turn off any feelings or hopes that he would one day have any contact with his father. He'd moved on and found other outlets for his emotions with the Legion. Now, any hopes that might have hovered in the back of his mind were washed away.

He came to the lawyers' office to collect his father's ashes, sign the required papers and assume title to the home in Barcelona and the villa in Mallorca, and receive power of attorney over the bank accounts his father had at the time of his death.

But also on his mind after visiting the scene of the accident, was whether or not his father may have had enemies. Someone who might have wanted his father dead, because the signs he saw on the roadway in

Cap-d'Ail told him a different story then the one reported by the locals and the Villa Gazette.

It had the air of something more deliberate. It had the stench of murder; and murder was something Lucas was intimately familiar with.

"Monsieur Charpentier, thank you for seeing me on such short notice," Lucas said as he entered the office. Like everything in Monte Carlo, the small office space was lavishly decorated. Marble floors, rich black leather furniture, and an antique desk from Provence.

"Of course, Lucas. I was very pleased to hear from you, and in fact, quite surprised that my correspondence found you through the Legion's headquarters. May I ask where you were stationed when you received the news?"

"I was in Corsica, and your letter was timed perfectly. My enlistment was coming to an end, and it gave me the purpose I needed to start my life over."

"I'm deeply sorry for your loss, Lucas. Your father and I were friends for many years."

"Thank you, I'm glad to know that. I never really knew any of my father's friends. I heard him speak a few times about the man he worked for at Banco Baudin, Monsieur Berger, but never anyone else, " Lucas said.

"I don't think Jean-Étienne Berger was much of a friend to anyone, let alone your father. I had to threaten him with legal action to get him to pay out the remainder of your father's commissions into his account after the accident."

Lucas thought carefully for a moment on his suspicions about the accident, "I thought they were on very good terms. Are you saying they were not?"

"I can't say that I know exactly what the nature of their relationship was, outside the work of the bank. But I do know that Monsieur Berger often forced your father to travel to places, and interact with people that were distasteful to him. A bank that performs the types of services for clients as Banco Baudin does, often deals with very unsavory people, and what they do for them is secretive and perhaps just as unsavory."

"By any chance, do you know who he was going to meet at the restaurant in Cap-d'Ail when he died?"

"No, I wouldn't. I must say that I found it odd though, the choice of restaurant where he was meeting a client."

"How so?" Lucas asked.

"Well, your father was every inch a true Spaniard; he detested traditional French cuisine. And the Blue Duck Restaurant in Cap-d'Ail is about as French country traditional as they come. To my knowledge he would have never gone there willingly, and virtually all of his clients were Middle Eastern, and they hate the food as much as he did. Someone must have really twisted his arm to make him go there."

"His boss, Monsieur Berger?" Lucas asked.

"Possibly. Very likely in fact," he said. "Speaking of odd things, I have something else for you besides the paperwork and your father's ashes. On that very same morning of the day he passed away, your father came by and asked that I include something into his private safe deposit box. It was a sealed letter, addressed to you. I hadn't put it away yet when I heard about the accident, and I kept it here in my desk."

He pushed his rolling leather chair back a short distance and pulled the center draw outward, and took out a letter sized envelope. It was crisply folded and golden colored, like one you might expect to contain an invitation to a royal wedding. He handed it over the desk to Lucas.

Lucas leaned forward and took it gently by the corner in the tips of his fingers, as though he were handling a piece of his dead father. It occurred to him this was likely one of the last things his father had touched before he died. "Did he tell you what's in it?"

"No. And I wouldn't ask. I'm sure it is something very private between you and him. But it did seem odd that he delivered it on that very day. I'm not a man who believes in things like premonitions, but it makes me wonder."

"It makes me wonder too," Lucas said.

"Will you be staying in Monte Carlo for any time?"

"I wasn't planning on it, but I think now, I'll stay for a few days. I might want to meet Monsieur Berger at the bank."

"If I might make a suggestion … Monte Carlo is a city where the quality of a man is often judged by his appearance. I have an open account at Boutique Zilli, and they have a fine assortment of clothing for men with athletic physiques like yours. Allow me to pay back some of your father's generosity to me over the years by setting you up properly with a suit for your meeting with Monsieur Berger, and few things for evening attire."

Lucas looked down at his shirt and pants and leather riding boots, all covered in eight hundred miles worth of highway dust and bug tar. He felt suddenly embarrassed by his appearance. "I'm sorry for coming in to meet you looking like this; I suppose after twelve years of living in battle dress uniforms and crawling through the dirt every day, I've lost my sense of fashion."

"Not at all, Lucas. I'm honored to be sitting with a man who has dedicated so much of his young life to serving France, and even more so considering you were not born a Frenchman. Please, I'll make a call to the manager of the boutique and tell him you are my guest, and whatever you need, he will take care of it. I will also make a reservation for you at the Hotel

Baston, near the sea. It's small and private, and within easy walking distance of everything, including the offices of Banco Baudin."

"Thank you, Monsieur."

Then the lawyer rose and walked to the bookcase along the front wall of his office, which extended to the ceiling and was full from end to end, and top to bottom with all variety of books pertaining to the laws of France and the micro-state of Monaco. More than a man could read and absorb in a lifetime.

On the fourth shelf at waist height, was a small wooden box. Plain, dark brown with a pleasant grain, polished to a semi-gloss finish and fitted with a single gold clasp to hold the lid. He paused for just an instant before reaching for it, and then turned to present it to Lucas with a respectful look on his face.

"Some people like to keep the ashes of the dead close at hand, but perhaps you'll want to spread your father's someplace special," he said. "It's a humbling experience, isn't it? To realize that no matter how great a fortune we might work to amass in this life, we are all destined to return to the most basic state; dust to dust as they say."

Lucas accepted the box in the palm of his left hand, and was surprised by how light it felt. His father had been large in his eyes; a powerful, bigger-than-life man that he once admired. And yet now, the contents of this little box represented all that he was. It didn't feel real.

He couldn't quite come to terms with this being all that remained of his father. He saw a light film of dust settled on the lid, and he wiped it away gently with his fingertips. He felt no connection at all to the remains inside, but the grain of the wood was warm and familiar. It took him a moment to realize why.

The natural grain from the little box reminded him of a polished rifle stock. Twelve years ago, he had traded the admiration he felt for his father for something else more powerful. Something that willingly put the power in his hands to right the wrongs that crossed his path. The fine, cool feeling of wood pressed against his cheek nearly every single day since, and often lay in bed with him at night. It was his most loyal friend and defender, and the two of them together were a force to be reckoned with. They were born for each other.

"I suppose it's better that I set his ashes free somewhere. I don't even know where I'm going to live just yet," Lucas said.

"Perhaps you might give his ashes to the sea. Your father loved the sea."

Lucas tucked the small wooden box and the large folder containing his paperwork, and the envelope from his father, into the top pannier of his motorcycle, and rode four blocks down the winding brick street from the lawyer's office to the posh storefront of Boutique Zilli.

He felt conspicuous as he stood in front of the polarized glass door and pushed the security buzzer on the panel, and glanced sheepishly at the camera, through which he knew he was being scrutinized. The door was pulled open wide, and a short slender man in his fifties, with a shaved and tanned head, wearing a brilliant blue suit and a broad smile, welcomed him into the store.

"Monsieur Martell! Please come in, I've been expecting you. My name is Bernard, and I am looking forward to fitting you properly for a business suit, and clothes for casual wear."

Over the next hour, Lucas endured having every inch of his body meticulously measured, and stood still on a raised platform in the center of the store as three assistants worked with Bernard, bringing color and material swatches and holding them against his cheeks and hair. They argued twice in rapid French over the difference between his waist measurements and his chest, and how difficult it was going to be to make the jacket fit without making him look like an ape. The men who frequented their store were not built with such a dramatic taper to their body.

When they were satisfied with their selections, Bernard released Lucas from the platform, "Monsieur Martell, I understand you are staying at Hotel Baston?"

"Yes. I'll be going there next to check in and take a needed shower."

"Excellent! I will have all of your clothing properly altered and pressed within two hours, and send them directly to your room. It has been a great pleasure being of service to you."

LATER THAT EVENING, Lucas was sitting in a large upholstered armchair in his third floor suite at Hotel Baston, looking out over the Mediterranean Sea and the hot pink sun as it slid below the waterline. The gold colored envelope was lying in his lap, exactly as it had for the past two hours since he first picked it up and sat down intending to open it. But the longer it stayed there, the heavier it got.

Lucas was a grown man now, and a decorated Legionnaire; he feared no one. And yet, even though his father was dead and he shouldn't have anything left to fear from him, he felt a gut-wrenching fear of what his father might have said in his last words to him. The words that were written and resting across his legs with the weight of an anvil.

His father's thoughts and his words still had power over him, as if he were still a seventeen-year-old boy. He imagined what they might be. Perhaps a final, scornful and malevolent rant. The final blow to remind him of his cowardice.

At midnight he reached for the crystal tumbler on

the marble table next to his chair, and poured the remaining finger of whiskey down his throat. "I'll read your final thoughts on my manhood another time, father," he said. He lifted the envelope and tossed it over to his bag on the sofa, and stumbled into the bedroom.

Chapter Nineteen

BANCO BAUDIN, MONTE CARLO

H e looked like a billionaire playboy. Or maybe a professional athlete who makes fifty million a year and buys ten-thousand-dollar suits for one date with a Norwegian supermodel. The suit was perfect in every detail, and the fit revealed just enough of his muscular frame to make him stand out from the boring millionaire crowd in Monte Carlo.

His desert combat tan looked smashing against the pale blue shirt, and the Legionnaire tattoos that covered his entire right arm and shoulder were now hidden from the world. The only thing missing was an exquisite timepiece, and maybe a single signature gold ring on his right pinky finger.

"Shit … who are you?" he said, looking at the mirror.

After making three phone calls, the hotel

concierge discovered the unpublished address of Banco Baudin, only three blocks from the hotel. "Shall I have a car take you to the bank, Monsieur Martell?" he asked.

Lucas laughed, "Why would I need a car? It's only three blocks."

"Most of our guests wouldn't walk such a distance in the morning heat, Monsieur."

"I'll manage, thank you," Lucas said as he turned and walked out into the warm sun.

As soon as he stepped out of the hotel lobby, he had the sensation of eyes upon him. It must be the suit, he thought; everyone can tell that I don't have any business wearing a suit like this. They know I'm faking it. But then the feeling came in a little stronger. He knew this feeling. It was the sense that someone was indeed watching him.

He'd felt this before, as he was patrolling with a squad through the villages in central Africa, and riding in Humvees with coalition teams through the streets in Afghanistan. It was his battlefield awareness sense telling him someone had him in their scope. This feeling had kept him alive more than once, and he had to resist the urge to seek cover.

As he walked the short distance to the bank, he kept to the shadowy side of the street, paused below awnings and sidewalk shade trees to catch a glimpse at the surrounding buildings. He ducked into an alcove between two luxury stores for two minutes in case he had a tail, but saw nothing.

BANCO BAUDIN OCCUPIED A RELATIVELY SMALL, two story office building in a private financial district of Monte Carlo. It was unimaginatively designed of concrete and stone on both floors, with only two windows on the second, and they were three-inch-thick safety glass with black glaze on the outside. It was impenetrable to gunfire, prying eyes, or high-tech listening devices.

There were no signs, no names, nothing that offered a hint as to the occupants of the building; only the street numbers, 3254. The only people who visited Banco Baudin in person were those who knew where it was, and had pre-approved appointments.

As Lucas dashed across the street and toward the building entrance, he felt the eyes that had followed him since he left the hotel replaced by others inside the building. The camera mounted at the top of the door spun slowly in his direction and followed his approach. He reached for the intercom button on the stainless steel panel to the right, but before he touched it, a deep male voice came over the speaker, "This is a private commercial business and we do not accept solicitors."

Lucas held down the button, "I'm not a solicitor,

my father used to work here, and I would appreciate a moment to speak with Monsieur Berger."

The voice responded as quickly as Lucas released the button, "No meetings without an appointment."

Lucas had prepared an answer, "Tell Monsieur Berger that he may speak briefly with me about my father's final commission payments, or Maître Charpentier will be filing for official investigation into the procedures of Banco Baudin. This can be as simple, or as difficult as he wishes to make it."

A long silence followed, and just as he was about to turn away he heard an electronic mechanism activate four sliding bolts in the door and it clicked open a fraction of an inch. He stepped to the left of centerline out of habit, and nudged the heavy balanced door open. Behind the door was a security entryway that measured barely eight feet square, with polished concrete floors, satin-finished steel walls, video cameras, and a walk-through metal detector.

A large man in a black suit and tie stood on the other side of the detector. The suit was stretched tightly around his gargantuan body, and only one button held the jacket fastened across his abdomen. He had no neck, but appeared as though his large, clean-shaven head was merely perched atop his square shoulders.

The guard didn't speak, but gestured for Lucas to pass through the detector. He stepped through and instantly the alarm sounded.

"All I have on me is the key to my motorcycle. Front right pocket," he said.

The guard motioned for him to hold his arms out, and he used a hand-wand to scan every inch of his body, twice going over the pocket which created an intense (*whaa, whaa, WHAAAA*) tone from the hand-wand. As the guard bent low to scan his legs and pockets, the snug suit jacket revealed the outline of a compact submachine gun strapped below his left armpit.

Again, the guard gestured toward the pocket without speaking, and Lucas reached in and pulled out the key and showed it to him. Then the guard nodded and pointed toward the door at the back of the security entrance, and as if it worked telepathically, it clicked open in the same instant. Someone else inside was carefully monitoring the activities in the entry.

Considering the austere exterior of the building and the top-secret security entry, passing into the lobby was like stepping through a veil into another reality. The floor changed from gray concrete to rose-colored marble, and the room didn't have the feel of a commercial lobby as much as it did a private salon in a mansion.

Lucas' eyes were first drawn to the fountain in the center of the room; octagonal with moorish tiles of blue and green and gold. Looking over the fountain he could see the back wall, covered in hand-cut travertine stone with the name, "Baudin", in large gold letters standing out from the surface. To the right, a private seating area with a large camel-colored sofa and two matching armchairs, and on the wall behind the sofa an original Claude Monet hung in a gold leaf frame.

A silky female voice spoke from behind him, "Monsieur Martell, please make yourself comfortable, and Monsieur Berger will be with you soon."

He turned and was snared in the gaze of a stunning woman. She was his age or perhaps a little older, black hair that fell well past her elbows in glistening waves, and eyes that defied any attempt to label them with a color. They were like Indian tourmalines, and the color intensified as she stared directly at him, and as the corners of her mouth drew into a smile, they faded to a storm-cloud gray. With every slight movement of her head, they changed, as did her demeanor.

From moment to moment she could be one woman, and then another. Her olive complexion gave her away as Mediterranean, but the eyes were like nothing Lucas had ever seen on the north side of the sea; but they reminded him vaguely of Eliza. He immediately considered she might be from the Middle East.

She was nearly as tall as Lucas, and slender with small round hips and long legs. She wore a crimson red dress that fit snugly around her thin waist and poured outward over her thighs, and tall black heels that made her calves firm and flex as she glided in his direction.

As she approached, he reflexively took a step backward; and as she smiled and stared into his eyes he blinked twice and turned his gaze away to the fountain. He couldn't hide his nervousness in the presence of extraordinary beauty. "May I offer you something while you wait? A Persian black tea perhaps?"

"No. Thank you, I'm fine," he said, looking further around the room to hide his flushing cheeks.

"Very well, it won't be a long wait; Monsieur Berger is anticipating your meeting."

Lucas turned and nodded his head in acknowledgment, and then walked to the seating area and took a chair that faced the Monet. As his head began to clear from the fluster, and the faint scent of her perfume faded from his nostrils, he thought about what she had just said to him.

How did she know my name? I didn't mention it to the security guard, and she didn't ask; she just knew who I was. His senses came back to him, and his battle-sense heightened. *They've been watching me since I arrived in Monte Carlo. Maybe even before.*

He stiffened in the chair and refocused on situational awareness. There was only one exit, which led back to the security entry and the armed guard before reaching the street. The only other he could see was an elegant Turkish walnut door on the opposite wall, behind the desk where the stunning receptionist sat. He assumed it led to the second floor, but had no idea if there were other exits from the building.

There had to be remote locking controls somewhere, and cameras that monitored both the entryway and the cameras on the outside of the building, and likely a team of operators and additional security. If things didn't go well, he was trapped in a kill-box.

He needed to keep his wits about him and play it smart. Don't threaten a man who has you trapped and vulnerable; be cordial. Extract information without interrogation, and get out alive.

"Monsieur Berger is ready to see you now," the receptionist said.

Lucas rose from the chair and turned to see her standing next to the walnut door, and as he walked across the room he heard the locks on the door snick open. Every door and every room were being closely monitored and controlled, as he suspected. The woman pushed the door open and stepped politely back, and as Lucas walked through the doorway she followed behind him and closed the door. The locks sealed with an audible "clack".

The hallway was long and elegantly decorated, like an art gallery. The overall lighting was dim, and recessed lamps in the ceiling spotlighted original works of art that hung on both sides. There were two doors, one on each side of the hallway, and one had a security panel on the outside with a fingerprint scanner. The security tech in this building was impressive. At the end of the hallway was a bronzed elevator with an accordion-style gate.

Lucas suddenly understood why his father's lawyer had suggested an appropriate suit for the meeting. He had grown up in a reasonably affluent fashion, but he felt as though he was entering a world beyond anything he knew existed.

He stepped into the elevator and could see his reflection mirrored on three sides, like an endlessly repeating image, and as he turned to face forward, the receptionist closed the gate and latched it. She smiled and lightly nodded her head as the elevator began to rise of its own accord, and she remained there, watching in the hallway until he disappeared to the floor above.

JEAN-ÉTIENNE BERGER WAS the shepherd of an incalculable fortune. Now in his early sixties, he was average height, but appeared shorter because years of sitting at a desk had lightly rounded his spine. He wasn't overweight, because he didn't really care much about eating, and had to be constantly reminded by his personal secretary to eat. She often brought food to his office, and instructed his housekeeper and cook at home to prepare meals even if he didn't ask.

His skin was the color of milk, as he rarely went into the sunlight, and recently it had begun to develop the texture of crinkled Japanese rice-paper over his hands and arms. The majority of his hair had left him many years ago, leaving only a halo of silver and a few wisps on top that waved lightly over his head when the indoor air-conditioning fan kicked in during the hot summer months.

He wore an expensive Italian suit every day, even on the weekends at home, because he often worked those days as well, from his home office. They were all dark blue, or gray. His only personal vice was the regular consumption of expensive cognac, and he kept a well stocked bar at his office and at home.

He lived in a small castle-like enclave on the cliffs looking out over the shoreline of Monte Carlo, and was the third generation Berger to serve as the President of Banco Baudin. He was born in Monaco, but spent most of his youth in the premier Saint Frances International boarding school in Geneva, before earning his Master in International Banking and Finance at the London School of Economics and Political Science.

In his final year at the university, he hastily married Louise Fitzpatrick, a rather plain looking young woman who he met in the library one Sunday afternoon. They courted and married without his father's blessing, and had a child within the first year, a daughter they named Sarah. He held her only twice in the first six months of her life, at Louise's insistence, but fatherhood didn't suit him well.

The day after his graduation from master's studies, he was called to return to Monte Carlo and begin his formal training in the investment bank that his grandfather had founded, and for which he would someday assume responsibility. His father insisted that Louise and the child remain in London, but they would be properly compensated. Jean-Étienne's life had been defined for him long before, and the error in judgment during his school years would not be allowed to interfere with his destiny.

Banco Baudin, despite the name, was not a traditional bank. Its origins were much darker, and its purpose less mainstream, along with the clients they served. It was founded in 1947 by Jean-Étienne's grandfather, Edmond, who relocated from Bern, Switzerland but was very likely not a Swiss native.

At the close of hostilities in Europe in 1945, a vast amount of wealth had accumulated in Switzerland, deposited in many forms; gold bullion, coins, works of art, and ancient treasures all hoarded into vaults by unscrupulous men. Some were Nazi officers trying to assure their personal finances after the war and others were politicians or businessmen profiting from the war, who needed to hide their wealth from the post-war reparations and asset seizures that would surely come.

But all of these men had a unique problem. How to convert their hidden assets into spendable cash without drawing attention. Banco Baudin became one of several specialized agencies that converted looted assets into real wealth, and shielded it from view. Accounts were opened without names attached, and transactions were strictly confidential, as provided for by the unique banking laws established in the micro-state of Monaco for just that purpose. It was a financial shelter from prying eyes.

As time passed, the variety of clients drawn to Banco Baudin's particular services broadened to include wealthy patrons in the Middle East and Far East, who wished to keep their wealth spread across many venues. And as the nature of the world changed, the bank's clientele slowly shifted from mere war-time criminals and profiteers, to include all of the vile enterprises that generated fantastic profits that needed a hiding place and generous interest.

They now shielded and moved assets for the Big Three of the underworld: Arms Dealers, Drug Cartels, and Human Trafficking.

Jean-Étienne's complexion was pale because he didn't like the outdoors and open air. He felt conspicuous and vulnerable, as if he was always under surveillance, which he likely was. He rarely sat outside on his beautiful terrace overlooking the sea, and he owned a magnificent yacht but almost never went aboard. He gazed at it through binoculars from his home office window.

He grew increasingly paranoid about his business and his associations, with each passing year, and as he handled more transactions for ruthless clients, he realized that someday his knowledge of their businesses would make him a liability to someone very powerful.

As THE ELEVATOR rose slowly from the art gallery hallway to the private office on the second floor, Lucas stood perfectly still in as relaxed a pose as he could. He knew he was being watched, and didn't want to create any sense of alarm. Looking through the accordion gate, his view changed from concrete and steel framing between floors to one of a large darkened room, and as the elevator came to a gradual halt, the gate clicked and drew back. He stepped out into yet another different world.

His eyes were first drawn upward to the ceiling which towered deceptively high overhead, with hand-painted frescos adorning the plastered surface, and a single crystal chandelier hanging from the center. The walls were French mahogany panels that wound in a circular arc on each side until they met in the center behind an enormous carved desk, and two black leather armchairs in front of it.

There were no windows in the office, so the two that were visible from the outside of the building had to be in rooms that were accessed from somewhere else. Along the circular walls hung even more works of art that Lucas could only assume were valuable, but he knew very little about art. He would have never guessed that the eight paintings in just that office had a combined worth of over fifty million euros; but half of them could never be traded on the open market, due to their illicit history.

Again, Lucas had the sensation of being drawn deeper and deeper into a dangerous place, with little chance of escape. He smiled broadly at the old man behind the desk as he walked into the office, and shifted his manner to appear subservient, and grateful for the audience.

"Monsieur Berger, I'm very happy to finally meet you in person! My father often spoke of you," he said.

Jean-Étienne looked up from his desk and seemed mildly surprised, and even relieved. Given the warning that Lucas had issued at the front door about the lawyer, he anticipated a more confrontational meeting. He stood and met Lucas in the middle of the room to prevent him from reaching the comfort of a chair, where he might want to overstay his welcome. He accepted Lucas' outstretched hand and wrapped his soft fingers limply around the hardened

Legionnaire's paw, but quickly let go and pulled his hand back. "How may I help you, Lucas?" he asked.

Not a pleasantry, not a condolence for the loss of his father, nothing. Lucas understood he was facing a man with no regard for others. "Allow me to apologize, Monsieur Berger; I may have reacted badly when your security guard addressed me at the front door. I just visited the place where my father died, and collected his remains. It has been very upsetting, as you can imagine, and I'm afraid I wasn't very polite."

The old banker didn't change his stance, "Understandable. But as I've advised Maître Charpentier, all the commissions and payments owed to your father at the time of his death have been fully deposited into his account. We have no further business to discuss."

"I believe you, Monsieur." He paused before deciding to ask the next question and possibly raise the tension level. "Monsieur, do you have any idea who my father was meeting at the restaurant in Cap-d'Ail the night he was killed?"

Jean-Étienne stiffened and raised his chin up to look at Lucas down the length of his narrow nose, "I most certainly do not! Your father's clandestine rendezvous were none of my concern. Perhaps he was meeting a woman he didn't want to be seen with in Monte Carlo!"

Lucas' caution went right out the window of the windowless room.

"Did you order my father to go to that restaurant? Because I inspected the accident scene, and it looks suspiciously like it was anything but an accident!" he barked down into the old man's face.

At the first hint of his voice raising above normal tone, a concealed panel in the circular wall flew open, and two men in suits rushed into the room. One seized him by the right arm and wrenched it quickly behind his back, the other grabbed his left arm and levered it to force Lucas up onto the balls of his feet and off balance. They were dragging him out through the open panel door and down a flight of narrow stairs in a flash. Jean-Étienne yelled as they pulled him from the room, "Throw the impudent trash out into the street!"

"I won't stop until I know the truth, Berger! I'll find out who killed my father, and I'll send them to hell!" Lucas screamed with fire in his eyes.

One of the guards slammed his fist hard into Lucas' kidneys, knocking the wind from him and choking his voice to a whisper. Then as they dragged him down the two flights of narrow metal stairway that wound through the concrete building, they alternately smashed his head and face against the wall, and his ribcage against the metal railing.

By the time they reached the bottom, his face was bloodied, he was losing consciousness, and he was gasping for shallow breaths. At the bottom of the stairs there was a solid steel door that automatically clicked open, and they threw him out into the garbage alley behind the building. He crashed headfirst into a dumpster and blacked out before hitting the ground.

BACK IN THE OFFICE ABOVE, Jean-Étienne was raging. He jerked open the top drawer of his desk and pulled out a private, fully encrypted satellite telephone, and frantically stabbed at the buttons to punch in a number. He was spinning in circles and stamping his feet, anxiously waiting for the signal to connect and ring to another encrypted phone that lived in another part of the world. After 30 seconds, the satellite links connected and he heard the rhythmic buzzing of the ring tone.

After five rings, he screamed out loud, "Answer the fucking phone!" but nothing happened. Beads of sweat were starting to form on his glossy forehead, and he was chewing his lower lip to the point of bleeding when he heard a click and a moment of silence, and then a male voice spoke in studied French with an odd, Arabic accent, "I am quite busy at the moment, Jean-Étienne. Why have you disturbed me?"

"I told you this would come back on us one day! I warned you!" the old man yelled into the receiver.

"Jean-Étienne, calm yourself and tell me what has happened."

"It's Lucas Martell; Francisco Martell's son. He was just here threatening me, he knows something!"

"What does he know? Did he provide any details?" the voice calmly said.

"He thinks someone murdered his father, and he said he won't stop until he finds out the truth! He needs to be dealt with now!"

"The son of Francisco Martell is of no concern to me, Jean-Étienne. He is your problem, and you need to take responsibility for it."

The old banker was out of breath and began to stumble for words, "But…but he said he was going to send us to hell!"

"Then I suggest you send him there ahead of us. And one more thing, Jean-Étienne; if you ever raise your voice to me again, I will send you to hell to keep him company."

The phone made two clicking sounds, and then fell to static white noise.

Chapter Twenty

MONTE CARLO

Lucas slowly opened his eyes, but all he could see was a palette of grays and browns. He blinked and tried to focus, and then realized he was lying with his face pressed against the street. As his senses came back, he could smell the greasy residue from the trash bin under his nose, and feel the sharp street grit pricking into the flesh of his cheeks and lips.

He raised his head and then pushed himself up onto his knees. He had a momentary rush of vertigo, his middle ears trying to readjust after being repeatedly slammed into a concrete wall. His lower back felt like a sharp spike was piercing his spine, and he thought one of the ribs on his left side might be cracked.

He grabbed the edge of the dumpster and pulled himself to his feet, wobbled for a second and then steadied. Then he felt the throbbing ache on the right side of his face. He touched one of his back teeth with his tongue, and it wobbled in the soft flesh. He could have easily pulled it loose from the jaw and thrown it away, but he decided to leave it be. Maybe it would reset itself.

He reached and braced himself against the side of the building, and slowly moved to the main road, pausing before he stepped out onto the sidewalk. He looked down and saw his expensive new suit, torn across the leg, and the hem of the jacket pulled out at the shoulder. *That didn't last long*, he thought.

He covered the three blocks back to Hotel Baston, feeling nearly recovered from the beating as he entered the lobby. The concierge looked startled when he saw him, "Monsieur Martell, are you alright?"

"Yes, yes, I'm fine. Just had a little fall on the street."

"Can I help you in any way? Would you like some aspirin or first-aid supplies sent to your room? I could even arrange for a doctor."

"Some whiskey would be nice. Can you arrange that?" Lucas said.

"Certainly, Monsieur."

Lucas went up to his suite and took off the torn jacket and threw it over the sofa that looked out to the sea in front of the window. He took a hand towel from the bath, filled it with ice from the mini-freezer and held it against his jaw, and stared out at the blue-green water. He was replaying the scene in the office in his mind, *That went ballistic faster than I thought it would. Something about me made the old man nervous. Very nervous.*

There was a light tap at the door, "Concierge, Monsieur."

Lucas opened the door, and the concierge was standing with a silver tray that held a bottle of Highland Park Eighteen Year Old Single, and two crystal tumblers. "May I, Monsieur?" he asked, gesturing to enter the room.

Lucas stepped back, and the concierge walked through and placed the tray on the table in the salon area of the suite.

"I see you brought two glasses, is someone joining me?" Lucas asked.

"I thought you might have a visitor, Monsieur; so I included another for your guest. The attractive young lady arrived shortly after you, and asked that I give you this letter in person," he said. Then he reached into his jacket and pulled out a sealed envelope, and handed it to Lucas.

"Will there be anything else, Monsieur?"

"No. Thank you."

After the concierge left, Lucas poured a finger of whiskey into a glass, sat on the sofa, and opened the letter. It was a short, handwritten note on elegant stationary from Banco Baudin.

It read,

.   .   .

"*Lucas, I am taking a great risk by reaching out to you. Don't speak to anyone about this.*

There are things you deserve to know. Things about your father, and also, about what happened to your sister.

I will arrive at the front entry of Hotel Baston at precisely 9:00 in a silver Range Rover. I will wait for one minute, and one minute only. I cannot afford to be seen in a public place with you, so we will drive and talk.

P.S. It would be unwise to ever return to Banco Baudin."

The pounding headache he had before was surging now, his pulse was thundering in his ears. *Eliza? How does what happened to Eliza twelve years ago have to do with any of this? And who is the woman*, he thought. No. Surely not the woman at Banco Baudin; Berger's private assistant. The notion made Lucas weak.

He'd been avoiding women for most of his adult life, and the brief encounter with this one had left him reeling. But then the content of the note sunk in a little deeper. What could she know about his father and Eliza? She had to know his father because he worked there and came to the office regularly between his travels. But what could she possibly know about his sister?

He looked at the clock on the wall table, it was 5:00. He had four hours to think it through, and come up with a plan, if this meeting turned out to be a trap.

LUCAS TOOK A LONG, hot shower; letting the steam soak into his pores, and the nearly scalding water loosen and numb the places that were sore from the beating he took at the hands of Berger's apes. He turned the water off, stepped out onto the cool tile floor, and wiped away the steam from the mirror. *I've been out of the Legion for three weeks, and my life is already going to shit*, he thought as he looked at the bruises and cuts on his face and body.

He had a faint afternoon shadow growing on his face, but he didn't feel like shaving again, so he just slicked his hair back and changed into fresh clothes. He put on the ivory colored slacks that Bernard had selected for casual evening attire, and a black silk shirt. It was warm outside, even in the night air, but he put on the light sport coat that matched the ensemble to hide the H&K pistol tucked into his right hip. He wasn't going out again in this town without a backup plan.

At 8:45 he went to the lobby of the hotel and looked out into the front entrance. There was a circular drive-through from the main road, and a roof that extended out to protect guests from the seasonal rains as they got in and out of vehicles. If guests or others wanted to park their vehicle, it was only available through the hotel valet. Lucas walked to the concierge desk, "Where does the valet park guest vehicles?" he asked.

"On the south side of the hotel, Monsieur."

Lucas walked through the hotel dining area and out onto the seaside veranda of the hotel, and to the right was a footpath leading to the valet parking lot. He walked through the lot containing two dozen cars and found, as he suspected, another path that came out through the garden to the front circular drive. He could remain in the thick planting of trees, completely hidden, with total visibility of any vehicle that came up to the front of the hotel.

At exactly 9:00, a silver Range Rover came in from the north on Princess Grace Highway and turned into the drive, pulled around under the covered entrance and stopped. He could tell the vehicle was kept in gear, rather than being shifted into neutral, and the driver was holding position with their foot on the brakes. Whoever it was didn't anticipate waiting there for very long.

The windows of the vehicle, like almost all others in Monte Carlo, were completely blacked out to protect the interior from the damaging sun, and the anonymity of the occupants. He couldn't tell who was driving, or how many others might be in the Range Rover.

He came in low on the passenger side of the Rover at a forty-five degree angle, which kept him just out of the driver's view from the side mirror. As he reached for the door handle with his left hand, he was also reaching for the .45 with his right. He snapped open the door and jumped into the seat in one swift motion, with the pistol held tightly against his waist and pointed directly at the driver. No one from the hotel, including the concierge who was standing at the front door, ever noticed the gun being drawn as he jumped into the car.

The woman behind the wheel, the same beautiful woman from the bank, had been focused on the front of the hotel and was startled as the door flew open and Lucas leapt in. She shrieked, and turned to see Lucas and the H&K pistol both staring at her with a cold ambivalence. Lucas glanced into the back and saw that she had come alone, "Let's go," he said. The dark haired woman drove out onto the highway and turned south.

For the past four hours, Lucas had been thinking about the note, and more specifically about Eliza. In fact he'd been reliving the events in Mallorca over and over in his mind, and fallen into a sullen mood. The woman's beauty held no sway over him now.

"Tell me your name," he said.

"Michele. My name is Michele."

"You said there are things I needed to know, so talk."

"Would you mind pointing that gun in another direction, you're making me nervous and I can hardly drive, let alone have a conversation," She said.

Lucas tucked the pistol back into the hip holster and fastened his seat belt, "Sorry, didn't mean to make you nervous. But the last time I was in the company of Banco Baudin employees it didn't turn out too well for me."

"I'm sorry that happened to you, Lucas. But you shouldn't have messed with Berger. He isn't a man you should trifle with."

"I'll keep that in mind. Tell me about my father; do you know who he was going to meet in Cap-d'Ail for dinner that night?"

"That's just the point, I wasn't aware that he was going there. Francisco came into the office that afternoon and he asked me to make a reservation at a restaurant here in Monte Carlo, and our driver was taking him there as far as I know. No one knows how he ended up on that road in Cap-d'Ail. I was standing in Jean-Étienne's office when the phone call came in from the constable, and I can assure you he was shocked by the news of your father's death."

Lucas had seen dozens of interrogations, and developed a generally reliable sense of when a person was trying to conceal information or outright lie. But Michele was difficult to read. He couldn't see any of the typical traces of truths or untruths that betray most people. The slightest movements of the eye or tensing in the corner of the mouth; the changes in respiration through the nostrils and subconscious licking of the lips. All of the normal tells were absent.

"Now tell me what you know about my sister, Eliza."

"I came to work at Banco Baudin when I was just nineteen years old. I had been here about six months when I saw your mother and your sister."

"You saw them? Here?"

"Yes, your father had a meeting with Jean-Étienne, and he brought them here. They waited in the salon while he was in the meeting."

"I think I remember that," Lucas said. "I was still in Barcelona taking final exams, and my father brought them here for a few days before we all went to Mallorca."

"Something else happened that day that might have been connected to your sister. When your father arrived with your mother and sister, Jean-Étienne was in a meeting with one of his most important clients, I believe he is an Arab, but I can't be certain. I don't know his name because, well, most of the clients here do not use their names. I have seen this man many times since, but still don't know who he is. Only that Jean-Étienne is always very nervous when he arrives."

"How is this man involved with Eliza's kidnapping?"

"I'm getting to that. This man came down from the upstairs office and left through the salon, and on the way out he stopped to shake hands with your father, but he never took his eyes off your sister. When you father went up for his meeting, this man stayed. He bent down on his knee and chatted with her. I've seen the way some men look at beautiful young girls. Look at them in a way that they shouldn't. Some men looked at me the same way when I was very young, and you never forget a thing like that."

The thoughts that Lucas had pushed to the furthest recesses of his mind, thoughts of what might have happened to Eliza after she was taken, began to pop uncontrollably into his head. For an instant, he also considered what Michele was telling him, and that she must have also been a beautiful girl who would have caught the eyes of predators.

He could tell by the way she spoke about it, that she had likely lived it herself. He felt a sudden wave of empathy for her, for what she might have endured, and the feeling caught him by surprise. He hadn't felt anything even remotely close to empathy for many years.

She continued, "After a while, the man left, but within minutes after your father left the office with your mother and sister, he returned. He went upstairs again, and while he was there Jean-Étienne called down to me and asked me look up the address of your father's home in Mallorca."

Lucas' head fell back against the soft leather headrest in the Range Rover, and his heartbeat was again drumming loudly in his ears. He stared blankly out the side window as they drove through the streets of Monte Carlo, with shades of neon greens, blues and reds flickering in through the windshield as they streamed past endless rows of casinos and shops.

The implications were mind boggling. His father's boss had possibly assisted in the kidnapping of Eliza. Jean-Étienne knew the man who did it, and that man was still doing business with him. And, his father may have known the man too.

He leaned forward and put his face into his palms, and then looked up again into the kaleidoscope of the city. Then it came to him, "I'm the only one left alive. The only one of my family that hasn't died from this thing. But now I'm strong enough to set it right."

He turned his head to the left to look into her eyes, but was blinded by a flash of headlights coming straight into the driver's side of the car.

THE WERE no tires screeching or skidding or warning of impending doom. The impact lifted the silver Range Rover into the air, and sent it into a slow, silent roll above the ground. There had been a single crunching explosion, and then the sensation of floating weightlessly in space, the seatbelts being the only thing that kept them from flying away. Their arms flailed first to the left, and the woman's left hand made a horrible 'crack' as it slammed against the door; then Lucas watched his arms floating out in front of him like he was in zero gravity for just an instant.

The driver's side window disintegrated into razor sharp fragments and ricocheted about the cabin of the car. Then the Rover came back to earth with a grinding howl as it landed on the passenger's side and slid across the highway. It came to a sudden stop against a lamppost, balanced on its side with the wheels spinning furiously until the engine locked up.

Michele was unconscious, her waist held fast by the seatbelt, and her upper body hanging limply down across the center console, her right hand laying across Lucas' lap. Lucas was laying against the door frame, with the pavement once again in his face through the shattered window, and his torso was still firmly held by the seatbelt.

His first instinct was to reach for his weapon, but his right arm was pinned between the weight of his body and the door, and the gun was jammed against his right hip. He put his left hand down on the pavement and the shattered glass fragments were digging into his palm.

He was struggling to push his weight up just enough to free his arm and reach his pistol when he saw the gargantuan figure in black standing in front of the windshield, and raising a weapon.

It was the same unmistakable goon from the security entry at Banco Baudin. He raised the gun with a long silencer attached to the barrel and took careful, deliberate aim at Lucas, but before he pulled the trigger, Michele came to her senses and began a series of blood-curdling screams. His attention diverted instantly to her, and he swung the weapon up to make his first shot silence the noise. That was the only break Lucas needed.

With a herculean push he pressed his entire body weight up with just his left arm, and pulled the H&K .45 with his right. As soon as it cleared the holster, he rotated the barrel forward and began shooting from the hip in rapid fire. The windshield of the Rover, undamaged until then, became splattered with holes and then frosted over in streaking spiderwebs.

The gun was empty in less than three seconds and the slide locked back, ready to chamber a fresh round as soon as it was fed another clip. The booming report of the shots echoed through the Rover. It was like being trapped inside an empty metal oil drum, and someone pounding it with a sledgehammer. Then thundering noise fell silent.

Lucas didn't remember popping the magazine release, nor pulling his spare from his front left trouser pocket and shoving it into the handle and chambering the next cartridge. His combat-conditioned subconscious worked fast and completely on autopilot. He sat quietly for a second, staring at the glistening webwork of glass and the rainbow of city lights reflecting through.

The eardrum-bursting gunfire had stunned Michele into a numb silence, and she was hanging down close enough that her long wavy hair was spread over him like a dark blanket. He could feel the wisp of her raspy breath as she stared at him with wide eyes. She was terrified.

The old agent's chant ran through his brain, "*If you're not shooting, you're reloading. If you're not reloading, you're moving. And if you're not moving, you're dying.*"

He reached down and pushed the belt release, and quickly spun upright with his feet under him, standing on the pavement through the right side window. "We've got to move," he said to her.

He held her body weight up and reached over and pushed the seatbelt release, and she fell into his arms. He turned her upright so she could get her feet under her, and felt the firm curves of her body sliding gently down against his, and her breasts brushing against his cheeks before her toes tapped the ground beneath her. They stood for an instant, compressed against each other in the tight space, and staring into each other's eyes.

He glanced at his pistol, pulled the slide back half an inch to see the reassuring shiny brass of a fresh cartridge in the chamber, and then pointed the gun forward. He punched the windshield with his left fist, and the safety glass decomposed instantly to pebble-sized pieces. The first thing he saw was the large dead body spayed out in front of the vehicle.

Lucas stepped quickly through the opening, out onto the street, and then lifted her out behind him. "Stay here for a second," he said.

He peered around the front of the Range Rover, and immediately it was riddled with automatic weapon fire from the belly-up side of the car. "Shit, there's more of them."

He looked around to his right, and saw that beyond the lamppost, the ground dropped off into a steep grassy hill, and at the bottom was another side street that was not well lit. Across that street was a dark alley that led straight to the seashore.

He could hear the waves of the sea lapping against the stone bulkheads in the darkness, and he knew they couldn't be far from the hotel, because they had been driving in circles. If they could make it to that dark alley, only an idiot with a death wish would follow him. The corpse laying out in front of the Range Rover was probably all the convincing the others needed to keep their distance.

He looked into her eyes, and now they appeared as dark as the night around them, "Can you move?"

"Yes, I think so."

"The grassy hill on the right looks like it's just been watered. It will be slippery. We can jump over the curb and slide down on our bottoms faster than we could run down. The shooters on the other side won't see us go. We'll be at the next street below and on the run before they know we're gone."

Her eyes widened at the thought that more men trying to kill them. She nodded her head, "Tell me when."

"Now."

He took her by the hand and pulled her with him as he leaped over the curb. They landed on their feet, but were quickly sliding at high speed on their backsides down the steep hill. It was thirty meters to the next street below, and they covered the distance in what seemed like seconds. As it leveled out at the bottom, they dug in their heels and bounced forward onto the their feet, bolted across the side street and down the dark alley.

Chapter Twenty-One

MONTE CARLO

T he pair came hobbling into the hotel from the dark terrace that looked out over the sea, which was shimmering under the light of a new moon. As they came through the lobby and headed toward the elevator, the concierge saw them and ran over.

"Monsieur Martell! Have you had another fall on the streets? The mademoiselle looks badly hurt! Should I send for the doctor on call?"

"Yes, please; and send up some dinner if you wouldn't mind. Anything you recommend." Then he added, "And one more thing; if any large men in black suits enter the hotel, ring my room and then hang up after two rings."

"Oui, Monsieur!"

The hotel doctor came to the room and examined both of them, pulling several shards of glass from the left side of her face, dabbing them with tinctured antiseptic, and wrapping a stretch bandage tightly around her left wrist and hand, "The glass left tiny marks in your cheeks, but nothing that needs stitches; use a good moisturizing lotion everyday, and you won't notice a single blemish within a week or so. I don't think your hand is broken, but you'd be wise to have it X-ray'd in the morning."

"I will, thank you doctor," she said.

AFTER THEY WERE ALONE, Lucas poured a glass of whiskey for himself and offered to pour one for her, "Would you like a drink? It might help calm your nerves."

"No, I don't drink alcohol, thank you."

"I can have the concierge bring up some herbal tea, if you like."

"Yes, that would be nice."

Lucas called downstairs and requested the tea and hot water. Then he opened the glass door out to the balcony, and the night sea breeze drifted in. It was cool and briny, and carried the fragrance of the Aleppo pines along the cliffs. The smell of the Mediterranean was always more powerful at night, and overwhelmed the senses. A lightly acrid taste in the back of the throat, with a hint of fresh fish on the tip of the tongue.

The air was warm, but felt cool as it swept across

the cheeks and over bare arms and legs, and the rhythmic rolling of the waves as they broke over the stone walls soothed the mind. The moon was full and cast a silver streak across the water, and the lights of the city above and behind the hotel sparkled like glitter on the breakwater.

Lucas was looking at the sea through the open doorway. He watched the ghostly shapes of people moving about the marina, and the endless array of yachts moored in the harbor, all lightly rocking to the rhythm. He loved the sea, it was the only thing he missed from his old life; and it made him think about Mallorca. As if on cue, Michele asked, "What is Mallorca like? I've never been."

Lucas turned toward her, "It's hot this time of year, but beautiful. The afternoon storms come in and pass quickly, and leave everything feeling damp and cool. The sea is warm and calm at night. I used to love swimming at night."

"I'd love to see it someday."

"Michele, may I ask where you are from? You have a French name, but your accent isn't French, and I hope this doesn't offend you, but…you don't look French."

She was holding the bandaged hand in her lap and lightly rubbing the sore wrist. She didn't answer him right away, as though she had been lost in thought and didn't hear his question. Then she looked up and said, "My name isn't Michele. I took the name

Michele when I was sent here to Monte Carlo to work for Jean-Étienne. Everyone who moves to Monaco eventually takes a more French-sounding name to blend in."

Her eyes were reflective and softer now, like the color of the afternoon sky as it wanes from blue to gray on the far horizon. She was wrapped in a thick white cotton robe with the Hotel Baston logo on the left breast, and her long, dark legs folded up beneath her on the sofa. The hair that earlier flowed like the mane of an Andalusian stallion was now twisted back and restrained behind her head.

She was still irresistibly beautiful, but not the fierce, confident beauty she displayed that morning; her heart was ever so slightly exposed. She looked directly at him, and he held her unwavering gaze as steadily as he might have gently held her face in his strong weathered hands. For the first time in his adult life, he felt a warm solace welling inside him from staring at a woman, rather than shame.

"My real name is Avigail. When I was little, my family called me Avi. I always liked being called Avi," she said.

"Avigail. Isn't that a Jewish name?"

"Yes, I was named after my grandmother. My mother was Israeli, from Tel Aviv; but my father was a wealthy businessman from Algiers. My mother died when I was very young, and my father took my sister and me to live in Algeria. It was very fortunate for us, because we were able to attend a private school and learn French, and several other languages, and when I left school my father had contacts in Monaco who were able to help me relocate here and find work at Banco Baudin." She paused and looked out the window into the dark sea, "But now it seems my employment at Banco Baudin has ended. What are we going to do, Lucas?"

"I would have normally cut my losses and slipped away from the battlefield. But after the news you shared with me in the car, I'm afraid Monsieur Berger and I have some unfinished business," he said. "I don't think you'll ever be able to rely on him for a reference."

They sat in silence for several minutes before Lucas spoke again, "Do you know where he lives?"

"Yes, of course. He lives in the home his grandfather built after the war, on the north cliff face of the harbor," she said. "It's an exquisite home with a beautiful view of the sea."

"Have you been in the home? Could you draw a basic map of the house from memory?"

"Yes, I've been in the home many times. Jean-Étienne is always working, he has an office there as well, and he often asked me to assist him on the weekends. I could make a very excellent map of his home. But, what are you going to do?"

"I'm going to make sure his private security team doesn't come back to finish the job they started with us. And then Jean-Étienne is going to share every detail he knows about my father and Eliza. Whether he wants to, or not."

Lucas slept late that night, and when he awoke the next morning stretched out on the sofa, he discovered a warm blanket draped over him. On the table in front of the sofa was a sheet of paper with a map of the house. Avi was gone. He was disappointed that she had slipped out in the night, the first woman he had ever been able to sit comfortably with and speak to without choking on his words. But there were other things to focus on now.

Lucas showered and dressed, and went downstairs to have lunch on the terrace. As he walked through the lobby, the concierge waved from his desk, "Monsieur, the mademoiselle left something for you."

"Did you see her leave?" Lucas asked.

"Oui, I called the private car to take her home. She asked that I inform you she was going home to gather some personal items, and she would return here by 9:00 a.m."

It was 12:30 now. Lucas thought for a moment, before asking, "Would it be possible to have the driver take me there?"

"Certainly."

.   .   .

LUCAS KEPT a careful eye on the surroundings and traffic from the back seat of the BMW 750i, as they drove from Hotel Baston to the outer perimeter of the city. There were tall condominiums and rental apartments scattered on the hillside with modest views and easy access. Most belonged to the service class of Monte Carlo residents.

The driver pulled up and stopped in front of a small, Austrian-styled cottage in a cul-de-sac of similar homes, "This is where I left the mademoiselle early this morning, Monsieur," the driver said.

"Wait for me, I won't be long," Lucas told the driver.

As he went up the short brick walkway to the cottage, he noticed that the front door was open a few inches. His right hand moved instinctively up and tapped the bulge of the pistol grip under his loose shirttail. He didn't want to pull the gun out in plain view of the neighborhood, but his subconscious mind wanted to know it was there.

He slowed his pace, and stepped lightly onto the first wooden step up to the porch of the house. He could see the second step was weathered and cracked and would likely squeak if he put weight on it, so he stepped over it and to the left of the front door. With his left hand, he put just enough pressure on the door face to move it open another foot. He waited and listened for sounds in the house, but heard nothing.

He bent his head slightly to peer through the glass

and around the door frame, it was dark and soundless; so he turned sideways and slipped through the half-opened door and drew his H&K immediately. He cradled the gun with two hands, and held it up in front and closer to his face than he would if he were in a wide open space. He didn't want it too far out front where it could be snatched from his grip. He kept the glowing orange front sight in his field of view, and swept around the living room and the open bedroom; then slowly moved through the only interior door, which led to the kitchen. There was no one in the house.

He flipped the light switch on the wall and as the overhead lamp flickered and came to full on, he could see the signs left by a violent struggle. A lamp lay smashed in the corner where it fell from the table; chairs pushed over on their side, and a rug pushed away from the entrance hall and up against the wall. And on the sand-colored hardwood floors near the front door, three drops of blood, splattered in a small triangle that looked like an arrow pointing the way.

Chapter Twenty-Two

HOTEL BASTON

L ucas opened the door to his room. It was completely dark and the terrace shades were drawn, which made it feel like a cave. He couldn't see a thing, and the light switch was far enough inside that he would have to enter the darkness to reach it. He thought he had left the lights to his room on and the shades open.

His first instinct was to retreat back into the hallway, but he ignored it. *I'm just getting paranoid*, he thought to himself. Housekeeping ignored my 'Do Not Disturb' sign and came in anyway, to clean the room. He stepped back through the door and fumbled with his hand along the unfamiliar wall until he felt the switch and tapped it. Nothing happened.

He stepped back again and put his hand on the pistol grip, he really was paranoid now; then the lamp next to the armchair against the wall clicked on.

"Your first instinct was accurate. You should have listened to it," Diggs said.

Even though he recognized him instantly, Lucas' heart jumped two beats when the light revealed the man sitting in his room. Had he been someone with really bad intentions, Lucas would have been dead.

"Jesus Christ, Diggs; I could have killed you," he said.

"You're playing in a new league now, Lucas. If you want to survive, you'll need to learn some tradecraft. That's one of the reasons I'm here. To teach you to survive."

"I didn't know I was playing at anything. The last week hasn't felt like much of a game to me."

"It *is* a game. A very complicated, devious, and deadly game; organized by people who live beyond the scope of the normal world. And most of the players, like you and me, never even know we're part of it," he said. "I swept your room for electronics and it's clean. Let's have a chat."

In 1972, William S. Diggs was among the brightest of Political Science majors at the University of Virginia in Charlottesville. He grew up in a small town, played tight-end on the high school football team, and went to the state finals on the varsity wrestling team.

In his final year, he had the highest SAT scores ever recorded in the history of his school, which earned him a full academic scholarship, and put him on the radar of a federal agency. In his senior year at UVA only months before graduation, things took an unusual turn.

Billy, as he was known by his family, was falsely accused of assaulting a young coed at a fraternity party. A fraternity that he neither belonged to, nor could anyone confirm that he even associated with any of its members. He claimed that he had been in his dorm room studying alone all night for exams when the supposed assault occurred, but he had no witnesses to corroborate his story.

He had very few friends in university, and generally kept to himself. After a series of official investigations by the local police department and the campus police, no formal charges were filed, but his scholarship was revoked and he was forced to leave school.

He ended up living back at home, and working at a small grain store loading fifty pound bags of livestock feed into the backs of pickup trucks, all day long. He was disgraced in the eyes of his family and the town.

Three months later, he was hitch-hiking home from work one day. A strange man in a Cadillac pulled up and gave him a lift home. That man was a recruiting agent for the Central Intelligence Agency.

Diggs spent the next nine months at the CIA indoctrination and training center at Camp Peary, VA, affectionately known as, "The Farm." They trained him in the basics of fieldcraft, weapons, interrogations, intelligence gathering, and the development and manipulation of informants. His first post was Cambodia, at the height of the Vietnam War.

Over the next four decades, he moved from the Golden Triangle to the jungles of Central and South America; the ancient cities of Eastern Europe and the Baltics, and finally to the hellish heat of the Middle East. Billy Diggs had joined the CIA with dreams of making a real difference in the world, and serving his country, but had instead become a man who manipulated, tortured, and killed without conscience.

He had reached a stage in his life when many wanted him dead, and he had little reason to fault them. And then, another mysterious stranger found him.

Throughout his years in the CIA, Diggs had come to realize that trying to keep millions of people safe was a flawed approach. It was easier to simply hunt and kill the few who would do them harm. His new benefactor gave him the chance to do exactly that.

LUCAS WALKED over to the desk and poured a small

glass of whiskey to calm his nerves, then sat on the sofa. "Alright, tell me what kind of game I'm playing in."

"When the Legion sent you to join a civilian team on a night raid to Algeria, what was your first thought?" Diggs asked.

Lucas sipped the whiskey and felt his dry throat clench as it burned its way down to his stomach, "I've been loaned out to other teams a hundred times. I speak four languages and I know my way around North African. And I'm a hell of a shooter. It didn't feel that out of the ordinary."

"Really?"

"Ok, I thought it was a little strange that it was a private mercenary team with an agent. But I figured you were CIA or something, and they were using non-US personnel in case shit went really bad. Plausible deniability, and all that. Am I right?"

"Not even close. The Tipasa mission was mostly an evaluation. An interview of sorts, for you. It's true we needed to eliminate the broker, and I wasn't anticipating the Tauregs had already done it for us; but we knew the girls were there. We were testing you to see how you reacted under the stimulus."

Lucas' eyes narrowed and his lips parted slightly to take in more oxygen through his mouth, the autonomic reaction to stress. "You knew the girls were there? Your men didn't look like they were interested in saving them. What were you planning to do with them?"

"Those men weren't really Fairhope Group employees. We subcontracted them from one of the dirty private security groups in Syria. We were going to extract the girls, but the real question was, how were you going to handle it?"

Lucas jumped up from the sofa and stared down at Diggs, "I fucking killed three men because you set up a test, that's how I handled it!" he yelled.

Diggs sat calmly looking up at Lucas. "I was there to assess your skills and reactions, but I'm not the one who set it up, Lucas."

"Then who did? Who's so damned interested in interviewing me?"

"I can't tell you that, because I don't know. I was given very detailed instructions on the operation, and asked to evaluate you as a potential operative. But this isn't a business where I know all of the principals or I'm privy to what they are planning. But whoever it is, they have a particularly vested interest in you. They wanted to make sure you survived the operation in Tipasa."

Lucas collapsed back to the sofa and folded into the thick cushions. He reached for the glass of whiskey, threw back the remaining liquid, and his expression faded from anger to bewilderment.

"Pour yourself another glass of whiskey and one for me, and I'll tell you as much as I can."

. . .

WHAT DIGGS SHARED over the next two hours completely disrupted Lucas' view of the world, and his own life. Diggs told him that only ten countries around the world actually make any attempt to track the number of reported missing children; and just among those ten countries, nearly one million children are reported as missing every year. The real number of children who disappear around the world and are never recovered, is staggering, and many of these disappearances are part of a multi-billion-dollar industry.

There is an international market for human commodities, and an organizational hierarchy that manages it. There are professional snatch teams working the streets, transporters and smugglers, brokers and auction markets, and many different levels of buyers from the low-level sex trade to clients willing to spend several million dollars for an exotic purchase. The industry co-mingles with a number of other highly profitable ventures, like the drug trade and arms dealing. There are wars funded almost entirely from profits generated by human trafficking.

There are banking networks that make fortunes just laundering the payments through their digital systems for five percent of the gross. They use dummy corporations, like real estate development and construction companies, to filter the foul-smelling profits of criminal enterprises like human trafficking. And the perpetrators protect their business by buying the cooperation of law enforcement, judges, and elected officials. There are even prime ministers and presidents on the payroll.

"So, what does Fairhope Group actually do? Is it about bringing these people to justice?"

"No, Lucas. Justice is about righting a wrong, and there is no possible way to right the things these men do. What Fairhope does is more fundamental. It's about retribution. We work by the oldest code, we bring the art of *vendetta* to evil men. Whoever the financier of Fairhope is, they gave us one directive regarding these people: hunt them, and kill them without mercy. We bring death to the ones we find, and fear to those we haven't yet found."

He paused for a sip of whiskey and let the words settle into Lucas' mind.

"Do you know if my father was involved in all of this?"

"All we know for certain is that Francisco's job for many years was helping the super-rich launder their profits from elicit businesses, including human trafficking. Whether or not he really understood what business they were in, we can't say. Personally, I believe your sister was taken twelve years ago as leverage, to keep your father's loyalty in line. Who knows, maybe he thought they would return her one day. A few weeks before the Tipasa operation, we received a tip that a gathering of high-level players involved in human trafficking was about to happen in Mallorca. It was only a few days after the tip-off, that someone assassinated your father. Which leads me to believe it was your father who tipped us off."

"I knew it wasn't an accident," Lucas said.

"No. It wasn't."

"Do you know who did it?

"I think so, but I can't be certain. All of the signs point to an assassin named Abd al-Rahman. He's an Arab, but in recent years he's been doing wet-work for clients in Morocco, Algeria, and Egypt. We think he may be branching out into political assassinations for Hezbollah."

"Why would those people be interested in killing my father?"

"Hezbollah needs money to wage war, and many of the large financial donors to Hezbollah are deeply imbedded in the human trafficking trade. He was probably loaned to them, just like the Legion loaned you to Fairhope. He's also likely to be in Mallorca three days from now."

"I want to be there when it happens."

'I thought you might."

"But… I have some unfinished business with Jean-Étienne Berger. There's a lot more to this story that I'm sure he knows, including the name of the man who kidnapped my sister, Eliza. I'm not leaving here until I get it."

"I understand. If I had the time I'd come with you, but I'm flying to Mallorca in five hours. I assume you know that his private security team intercepted your lady friend, his private secretary, this morning and took her to the mansion. I wouldn't expect her to be alive for very long, and you'll need a support team if you plan to go in there."

"I have one," Lucas said.

Diggs reached into this jacket pocket, pulled out a cellphone and handed it to Lucas, "This is an untraceable burner phone; keep it in your pocket at all times. It has one number stored in speed dial, that will ring through a voice recognition screen, and then forward your call directly to me. When I know more about the Mallorca meeting, I'll call you." Then he added, "I hope you get what you're looking for from Berger."

Chapter Twenty-Three

◈

D iggs sat in his car outside the hotel and made a call.

The telephone rang only once, before an electronically altered voice answered, "How is Lucas?"

"Berger's security team attempted to take him out last night when he was with the girl. They failed. Lucas handled himself very well."

"Does he know who the girl is?" the voice said.

"No. She left the hotel early this morning and went home, but Berger's team intercepted her there. Lucas knows they have her. He's planning to go in tonight."

"Will he survive?"

"Yes, of course. He's good at this. He'll be fine against the banker's security detail. But there's another problem; Abd al-Rahman."

"What about him?"

"He's here in Monte Carlo. I don't know where, but I'm sure he's watching. If he interferes, that considerably stacks the odds against Lucas surviving the encounter," Diggs said. He waited for it to sink in, and then added, "Should I provide support?"

There was a moment's hesitation, "No. Let's see how he handles it. The Mallorca gathering is just 72 hours away; if you kill Abd al-Rahman now then we'll lose everything."

"Confirmed."

Chapter Twenty-Four

A t 1:18 p.m., Lucas walked into a small kiosk on Rue Grimaldi and purchased a different disposable prepaid cell phone. He made a call to Céret, France. The receiver picked up after three rings.

Lucas said, "I need my guardian angel to watch over me."

Serge responded, "I thought you might. My gear is already loaded. I'll be on the road in five minutes. I'll take the A9 and A8 straight along the coast and be in Monte Carlo in under 5 hours. Where do we meet?"

"I'll text you the GPS coordinates."

THE SUN in July stays up a long time over the

Mediterranean, and Lucas had no intentions of coming into the kill-box that would surely be waiting for him at Jean-Étienne Berger's mansion, in broad daylight. He realized that every passing hour put Avi's life in greater danger, and he didn't take that lightly, but a poorly executed assault against a large and well armed force would be futile, and suicidal. He was going to let them stew, keep them waiting until long after darkness had fallen and when they started to relax, he'd come in hard and fast.

He did his reconnaissance on Google Earth satellite photos, and found a rocky, elevated ridge only four-hundred yards from the mansion, that would suit Serge for cover fire. There was only one long road into the property which he had to assume was being watched, so they took the Avenue Lavrotto two miles past the turnoff, tucked the car into the trees, and made a creep over the ridge through the dense thorny brush.

By 8:00, Serge was settled into his "Angel's Cloud" with a view of the front and western side of the house, and began collecting his shooting notes. He used a laser range-finder to get the precise distance to targets, calculated the elevation drop, and checked the temperature and wind drift. He adjusted his rifle scope to match the data so he could shoot at "dead zero".

Lucas continued his careful approach for another hour, and when he was two hundred yards from the house, he held his position in a blackberry thicket and waited for darkness.

Two guards came out of the front door to the mansion and moved to the front gate at 8:30. From his elevated perch, Serge could see another guard inside who came periodically to the front door and then the side window to peer out into the garden. By 9:30, the two at the gate were showing signs of being anxious, and began making radio calls to someone back at the house every five minutes.

The sun fell below the horizon at 9:48, and at 10:00 the automated lights in the park grounds came on as visibility waned. There were two large flood lights at the gate which made the guards easy to see through a rifle scope, and a series of lights in the manicured boxwood hedge that bordered the winding driveway to the house. In front of the house, four lamps lit the entry; but the sides and back were in near darkness.

The mansion had been built in the late 1940's on a remote piece of property. It had relatively easy access to Monte Carlo, a beautiful view of the sea, and was backed up to staggering cliffs and rugged terrain which was thought to be impenetrable at the time.

It was Bavarian in style; the foundation and lower level made of hand carved stone. They were a silvery granite with flecks of green and rose that sparkled when the sun was low in the afternoon sky, and were precisely fitted and mortared to last for many generations.

The upper level was hand-hewn cypress with a peaked roof to cast off the snow, even though it never snowed in Monaco. All of the windows had criss-crossed framing and thick leaded glass panes. The front of the property was a lush green garden with exotic plants and trees, and a manicured terrace that faced the sea, surrounded by an Italian balustrade.

The typically Germanic style of the house always seemed out of place on the Mediterranean shore, but it was a perfect reflection of its owner. The electrical system, lighting, and alarm systems were all upgraded over time, but the builder's thoughts on which direction a threat might come from remained the same. The subsequent generations of Berger's were more concerned with tax collectors or legal investigators arriving through the front gate, rather than an armed assault.

Lucas began to slither closer to the mansion under the cover of darkness.

By midnight, the two men at the front gate, each of whom weighed over two-hundred and fifty pounds, were beginning to feel the effects of standing on their feet for several hours, and carrying heavy weapons strapped to their bodies. Serge and Lucas could see them shifting their weight from one leg to the other; flexing their knees, and rubbing their thighs to stop the pins-and-needles of blood pooling in the extremities.

One of the guards kept pulling his jacket sleeve back to glance at his watch; first every ten minutes, and then in shorter and shorter increments. Lucas could tell he was going to move away from his post very soon, either to use the bathroom, or piss in his pants.

Finally, the guard pulled a radio from his pocket and made a frantic call to the house. A moment later, the front door opened and another guard in a black suit and tie stepped out under the front lights. He signaled for the guard at the gate to come back to the house and relieve himself.

Jean-Étienne must be sensitive about people pissing in his garden, Lucas thought to himself, as he was now lying beneath the English ivy along the edge of the house. He was only a hair's breadth from the front door.

As the guard walking back drew closer, Lucas pulled his knees up under him and dug the tips of his boot toes into the soil for his leap.

The guard stepped up onto the first stone steps to the front landing and exchanged a laugh and a joke in a Swiss-German dialect with the guard who came from inside. He grabbed his crotch and made a grimace with his face. It was the millisecond of distraction that cost both of them their lives.

Lucas rose up to a crouch, the pistol coming up fluidly at the same instant, and fired a round through the right ear of the guard who came from inside the house. He was less than ten feet away, and at that distance the .45 caliber bullet nearly vaporized his skull. His large body held motionless for half a second, and then it collapsed and sprawled across the stone floor like a gelatinous mass.

It's one thing to see something gruesome when you expect it to happen, and another to be caught by surprise. The guard grabbing his crotch in the middle of a laugh, was stunned by what happened just an arm's length in front of his face. Blood and tissue splattered all over him. His eyes bulged and a girlish screech slipped from his throat. By the time he started moving his hand to the machine-gun under his arm, Lucas was taking careful aim at his chest. W*hump-whump,…whump*. Lucas fired two rounds from the suppressed H&K rapidly into his chest, and followed with a third, precisely between his eyes.

Serge was watching the action intently through his scope, and the left corner of his mouth pulled up into a wry smile. He shifted his aim quickly to the front gate, where the remaining guard had heard the faint sound of the steel slide on the H&K as it clacked back and forth under fire, and he was pulling his gun up to the shoulder. Serge settled the center dot onto his chest, and squeezed the trigger.

The rifle recoiled fiercely into his shoulder and jumped off the backpack it was lying across. He lost focus on the guard for an instant. He came back on target, and saw the guard lying motionless on the ground.

Lucas moved quickly against the wall next to the open front door, and waited. He heard nothing moving inside the house, and he darted his head forward and quickly back, to catch a glimpse through the opening.

Machine-gun fire immediately shredded the door frame, and stone chips and glass sprayed over him as another guard in the house opened fire. The outer walls of the mansion were two-feet thick and solid stone, so they shielded him from bullets passing through, but he was pinned down. If he moved into the doorway he was dead meat, and if he moved to his left in front of the window it was just as bad.

Serge could see his dilemma, and he scanned the windows for any sign of the shooter. Gunfire erupted again, and through the side window of the house he saw the muzzle-flash of the weapon, but the shooter had taken cover behind a large iron wood stove at the far end of the salon.

"You really think you're safe there?" he chuckled. "Not from Serge."

He slid open the bolt on the sniper rifle, reached into his front jacket pocket and pulled out an armor piercing cartridge with a glowing orange tip. He held it up, gave the brass casing a gentle kiss for luck, chambered the round and closed the bolt.

He had a clear view of the front of the iron

stove at an angle through the window, but he couldn't see the shooter. He'd have to make an educated guess, and also anticipate that the angle of the window he had to shoot through, and the angle of the iron stove might shift the path of the bullet. He held his aim low and three inches back from where he thought the biggest part of the shooter's body was hidden.

He took a deep breath, slowly let half of it out and held it until he could clearly feel his own heartbeat throbbing in his neck. He could see a slight wobble in the reticle dot of the rifle scope as just the movement of his pulse quavered through the stock of the rifle. From this distance, a quaver was the difference between a hit or a miss.

The shot had to be perfect. He timed his trigger release between his heart beats, which were now thundering in his ears, and sent the blazing hot round down the mountain side.

Lucas heard the window glass shatter and the metallic '*BRRANG*' as the bullet struck the iron stove and bore a hole perfectly through and out the other side. A second later, he heard the muffled report of the big rifle echoing down the cliff.

Once again he darted his head quickly for a peak inside, and back again. He didn't see anything, but there was no explosion of gunfire either. He turned sideways and moved his head just far enough to see around the door frame without exposing his whole head, and saw the mangled form on the floor and the wall behind painted crimson red.

Lucas had the map of the house etched in his mind as he rushed through the front door, sweeping the pistol in front of him left and right for threats. He knew most of the rooms were on the first floor, with only the master suite and Jean-Étienne's private study upstairs.

The interior floors were golden pine and finely waxed, and his boots slid smoothly and silently over the surface. The salon was decorated with a woman's touch, with victorian antiques and tapestries that covered the stone walls.

He turned to the right, into the grand living and dining hall, with dark rosewood panels and more original masterpieces hanging on the walls. Lucas moved swiftly past the million-dollar artwork, without notice, and entered and cleared the kitchen, storage, and house-keeping quarters. Jean-Étienne had apparently given everyone the day off except his private security team.

Now Lucas moved to the winding spiral stairs that led to the second floor, staying to the outside edge of the passage with his eyes and pistol trained intently on the open space above him as he circled upward. He expected to encounter another guard somewhere on the stairs, but it was empty.

Lucas and Serge had each killed two guards, and one from the previous night during the car assault made five. Five was a typical private security detail; two for days, two for nights, and a driver. *We might have gotten them all*, Lucas thought.

At the top of the landing, there was a short hallway with a floor-to-ceiling window at the end, and two doors directly across from each other. One led to the master suite, the other to the study. He had to pick one door and go in fast, and expose himself to attack from the other side, if he chose wrong. He chose the left, moved against the wall and reached carefully for the door handle; turned it just until he felt the mechanism release, and then burst through with his shoulder.

Two steps into the suite, he realized he picked the wrong room but he was committed. He swept left and right, dropped down to check under the high post bed, and into the bath. Nothing.

He spun around to face the door, and standing in the hallway with a gun to his shoulder and aiming at Lucas was a sixth guard. Lucas felt his heart skip, as the guard pulled the trigger on his compact Steyr rifle, and heard a deafening "*click.*" The guard fumbled for the safety release with his thumb and was about to pull the trigger again when Lucas fired and kept firing until his H&K was empty.

When the hazy blue cloud of gun smoke cleared, the man's body was sprawled on the floor. Still holding aim on the corpse, he subconsciously triggered the magazine release; it popped out of the pistol, and before it bounced on the wood floor he was pushing a fresh magazine into the bottom of the handle. He moved quickly to the doorway, swept again to each side of the hallway, and then ran straight into the open door to the study.

Jean-Étienne Berger sat frozen at his desk with an indignant scowl on his face. His entire security detail had been killed, he was staring down the bad end of a pistol, and still his arrogance held the ground. He believed he was untouchable.

Lucas glanced to his left at Avi, who was sitting on the floor against the wall. Her face was bruised and her blouse blood-stained.

"Are you alright? Can you walk?" Lucas asked.

"Yes. They beat me. They wanted to know what I told you," she said.

Jean-Étienne snapped back, "It doesn't matter what she told you, it's all a lie. She doesn't know anything!"

"I'm more interested in what you know, Jean-Étienne," Lucas answered. "Avi, get up and go downstairs and wait in the salon. You'll meet a strange little man with a large rifle, his name is Serge. He's a friend, but he's a nervous sort so don't make any sudden movements around him. Jean-Étienne and I have many things to discuss, and this might take a while."

He kept his pistol trained on the old banker with his right hand, and reached down to Avi with his left.

She took his hand, and he pulled her effortlessly to her feet. She stood close to him, and he turned for an instant to look into her eyes. They were swollen and stained with fear. He could see the remnants of a man's knuckles lingering on her fine skin, and the indomitable character he carried into battle began to crack. His blood was boiling. Avi touched him lightly on his shoulder, then shot a piercing glance at Berger before she turned and left the room.

Chapter Twenty-Five

J ean-Étienne awoke in darkness, his eyes blurred with the sticky salty residue of dried tears and blood. He struggled to pull them open and tried to reach up to wipe them free of the goo, only to discover that his arms and hands were completely immobile. He felt his upper body pressing firmly against a hard, cold surface, and the weight of his hips and legs dragging at his lower back.

His vision came slowly, adjusting to the low light, and he saw that his arms were stretched out in front of him, and beyond them he could see the portrait of his father hanging on the north wall of his office. He was tied over the top of his exquisite Turkish walnut desk, with his legs hanging down over the side and each ankle tied to the opposing clawfoot. He was stripped completely naked.

"Come back to me Monsieur Berger," Lucas whispered in his ear. "We still have things to discuss."

"What? What? What are you doing to me?" he whimpered.

"You were about to tell me the name of the man who ordered my sister to be kidnapped, but you had a bit of a fainting spell," Lucas said. And then he leaned over into Jean-Étienne's field of view, and smiled.

"Man? What man? I don't know what you're talking about!"

"Oh, I think you do," Lucas said. Then he began to slowly stalk along the walls of the grand office, stopping to gaze at the paintings of each successive generation of the Berger family.

"I've made some inquiries while you were napping, Jean-Étienne, and discovered that your grandfather came here to open this bank from Bern, Switzerland just after the war. This was him, yes?" he said, pointing to one of the portraits that hung in a gold flaked frame against the mahogany panels. "But there doesn't seem to be any evidence of where the fortune came from that he used to fund the enterprise. Stolen Nazi gold, perhaps?"

"Lucas I have no idea what you're talking about. Release me at once, or you'll spend the rest of your life in a prison cell!" Jean-Étienne screamed.

"Are you familiar with the CIA tactic of waterboarding?" Lucas said, calmly. "It's a beautifully inventive interrogation technique. Delivers results very expediently, and leaves no lasting scares or physical harm. The agency had to come up with something that was difficult to prove, after the fact."

Jean-Étienne twitched nervously and wrenched his head around to see Lucas as he continued to pace around the shadows of the room.

"What kind of nonsense is this! Are you threatening to torture me now?"

"I've made no threat at all, I'm just having a polite conversation about retrieving information from someone who really doesn't want to give it to you. You see, during the past few years, I've had the chance to witness a great many of these, and become something of an expert," Lucas said. "I've watched the masters of enhanced-interrogation take battle-hardened men, men who are much more durable than you Jean-Étienne, and reduce them to quivering little birds that sing any tune you wish."

"You're going to waterboard me? Here in my own home? That's madness, Lucas! I don't know anything about what happened to your sister!"

"I didn't ask you about Eliza, I'm asking about the man who ordered her to be taken. And no, I have no intention of waterboarding you," Lucas answered. "Waterboarding requires some help, and it's messy. And I really don't give a shit whether I leave any scars or inflict permanent damage on you."

The arrogant rage in Jean-Étienne's face faded,

and the redness in his bald pate began to pale as a hint of fear forced the blood to retreat from his extremities.

"Your caretaker has a very well equipped workshop behind the garage, Jean-Étienne, you should be proud. I found exactly what I needed. Can you feel it? That slender, cold metal object inserted deeply between the cheeks of your soft ass?"

The old man's eyes widened and he started to squirm against the wire that bound his arms and legs to the desk.

"It's a soldering iron; an old-school CIA interrogator. It's plugged into the primary power outlet under your beautiful desk, and when I make my way around to the office door, I'm going to flick on the power switch," he said, as he leaned over again to stare coldly into his face. "Three seconds after the lights come on, you'll start to feel it warming up. Ten seconds later...well, you really don't want to know what you'll feel then. Once I reach that door and flip the switch, Jean-Étienne, I'll keep on walking because your screaming won't be of any use to me."

Lucas smiled again, and then straightened up and took one last look out the window at the Mediterranean Sea, glistening black and silver with refracted moonlight. He started walking towards the door.

"Lucas! I told you I don't know anything!" Jean-Étienne yelled.

Lucas kept walking.

"Lucas! Lucas, they'll kill me!"

"Who will kill you?" Lucas asked, but he never stopped walking toward the door.

"Lucas, please! Alright, I'll tell you who he is!" Jean-Étienne sobbed.

Lucas paused, his finger now resting beneath the light switch on the wall, and looked back as the old man craned his head in a desperate attempt to see.

"Lucas, I'll tell you who he is; and I forgot to tell you about the money!"

"What money?"

"Your inheritance! Your father has an investment account with a fortune in it! It's yours now that he's dead. I was going to tell you about it but … it slipped my mind."

JEAN-ÉTIENNE SAT in the large green leather chair behind his desk, wrapped in an elegant French night robe. The corners of his eyes and mouth sagged, and his thick grey eyebrows flicked nervously like long cat whiskers. The look on his face seemed a mix of resignation and desperation. Resigned to the fact that his life may be about to end, and desperate to find a way out of it.

Lucas came back to the desk and placed a Czechoslovakian crystal tumbler with two fingers of cognac in front of him, and another for himself on the other side of the desk as he sat in one of the guest chairs facing him. Next to the cognac he laid his compact H&K USP pistol, with the muzzle directed conspicuously at Jean-Étienne's round belly. He leaned back in the chair and opened the conversation.

"Tell me about the Arab. Leave nothing out. Who he is, where he can be found, and why he wanted Eliza. If I sense at any point you're lying to me or holding anything back, you're done."

Jean-Étienne reached for the cognac and poured the entire contents into his mouth. His throat was dry and raw from the yelling and sobbing; he swallowed hard with an audible "gulp," and winced as the liquid burned his trachea on the way down. He began to weave an intricate tale with the few details he knew.

"First, he's not an Arab. He lives in Algiers, so I assume he's Algerian. His name is Farouk Kateb, or at least, that's who I have always known him to be. These men often use an alias in their financial dealings, so I only know the name they use when they communicate with me. They do not have to attach a name, nor prove their existence in order to open a brokerage account with Banco Baudin. We have developed a reputation over the decades as an absolutely discreet institution that will wisely invest and protect assets for clients, without the normal burdens imposed by western nations. Farouk has been an account holder here for many years, and he has assets that are beyond the imagination of most men. The minuscule commissions alone, that we charge to service his accounts, make a fortune for the bank."

"Do you have contact information for Farouk?" Lucas asked.

"No. Farouk preferred to set up a numbered account that is managed entirely through electronic access, and once a year he makes a personal visit to discuss his assets and investments with me directly."

Lucas made a few notes on the desk pad, using Jean-Étienne's 18 carat gold Mont Blanc pen, and then asked, "How was Farouk Kateb involved in Eliza's kidnapping?"

"I don't know that he was!" he said. He was still grasping at a small chance to avoid betraying his client.

Lucas reached up and lay his hand over the grip of the pistol, "I warned you about lying to me. Are you sure about that?"

"Farouk was here in my office the day that your father stopped by with your mother and sister. We concluded our meeting, and he left. He came back, maybe thirty minutes afterward, and asked about the man, your father, who was waiting to see me in the lobby. I didn't think anything about it, I told him his name was Francisco Martell, and that he was a client manager for the bank. He didn't say anything more, he just thanked me and left."

"He didn't want to know anything else?"

"Nothing, I swear to it."

LUCAS MADE a few more notes on the pad, then took a slow sip from the cognac. "Tell me about my father's account. Why am I just now hearing about this?"

"Francisco opened a privately numbered account several years before the incident with your little sister. He made some healthy deposits from time to time; as you know, I paid your father extremely well for his services, and he received bonuses based on the earned commissions of his clients. I suppose he was planning for the future of his family in a way that would not be heavily burdened by the tax laws in Spain. After all, those pirate Spaniard politicians want thirty percent of every euro you earn."

He paused and cleared his scratchy throat, "May I have a bit more cognac, please?"

"Sure," Lucas answered. Then he stood and walked to the rolling bar and retrieved the decanter, glancing back as he walked away to see if the old man had any interest in going for the pistol that sat on the desk in front of him. The old man's eyes flickered across the path of the gun briefly, and then darted away as if the sight burned his eyes like looking directly into the sun. Lucas walked back, poured another bit into Jean-Étienne's glass, and then more into his own before taking his seat.

"How much money is in this mystery account?" Lucas asked.

"I'll pull it up for you right now."

He opened the folded computer lid on the desk, plugged it into a private server connection, and began to type. "Ah, here it is," he said. Then his eyes opened widely in surprise.

"How much?" Lucas asked again.

"Again, I had every intention of making you aware of this account. I was just taken back a bit by your manner the other day, and it slipped my mind. I can't imagine why your father wouldn't have mentioned it to you."

"I understand. Now how much is in the account?"

"At the close of business today, the balance stands at seventy-eight million, four hundred and sixty two thousand euros."

Jean-Étienne looked up from the computer screen, nervously chewing on his lower lip, and feigned a professional smile. "That should hold you over quite well, I would think?"

Lucas came around the desk and stood over his shoulder to look down at the account ledger, and there it was in plain text: €78,462,001.00.

"Where in the hell did all that come from? He never made that much money working for you!" Lucas said.

"Lucas, understand that this money has been sitting in this account for twelve years. Untouched, untaxed, and compounding with significant annual earnings," Jean Étienne said, as he turned and looked up at him. "And now this is all yours."

Lucas thought silently for a moment, "How do I access the money?"

"I can give you a list of the landing accounts, as there are several, spread out across four countries with favorable reporting regulations, and the main brokerage account here. You can sit and change the pass codes right now, and then you will be the only person who can access the accounts from anywhere in the world."

Over the next thirty minutes, Lucas changed and recorded all of the pass codes and made detailed notes of the account locations and numbers. As he made changes to the last one, the primary brokerage account at Banco Baudin, he took the time to scroll back through the deposit and earnings statements.

Year after year, the statements reflected similar events. Two deposits per year, usually in the neighborhood of two hundred thousand euros, which corresponded to his father's biannual commission bonuses. It was nearly identical all the way back until the year 2006.

In October, three months after Eliza was taken, and not long after Francisco Martell returned to his work at Banco Baudin, a single wire transfer was made into his account. A very large transfer. The sum was an even ten million euros. After that large deposit was made, with the account accruing an average of twelve percent a year and compounding, it was little wonder the balance had grown to an astonishing sum.

"Did you forget to tell me something else about this account, Monsieur Berger? The wire transfer of ten million euros in 2006, it came from another account in this bank."

Jean-Étienne's heart sank into his stomach. He knew his only hope of surviving now was to tell him everything.

"Yes. It came from Gibraltar Sea Lanes, a fishing vessel consortium," He said.

"Who owns Gibraltar Sea Lanes?" Lucas asked, reaching up again to embrace the H&K pistol still resting on the desk.

Jean-Étienne paused, then said, "Farouk Kateb."

Lucas was standing now, turned and staring blankly out the window into the dark night. The moon had crawled behind a curtain of clouds, storm clouds that were gliding in to bash the Monaco coast at any minute. He couldn't see the shimmering waves or any trace of the sea, all he could see was the empty void, like the obsidian blackness he felt sinking into his heart.

"Why," he asked. "Why would Farouk transfer that amount of money to my father?"

"It's not my place to ask about such things, Lucas. It's not my concern. But if I had to speculate, I would say it was compensation."

"Compensation for what?"

Jean-Étienne could feel his grip on life slipping away now, as if he were about to be splayed across the Turkish desk once again.

"These men, they exist in a different world than the rest of us, Lucas. I've seen them pluck twenty million euros from a briefcase to pay for a horse on a whim, as easily as you might buy a chocolate bar on impulse at the checkout counter in a grocery store. If they want something, they buy it without regard for price. If it's not for sale, they steal it. They believe themselves to exist in the realm of the gods, and gods are not bound by the normal laws or moral codes of average men. I think your father might have discovered something in his travels, or from one of his many wealthy clients in the Middle East. Something that made him believe that Eliza was alive, but would never be coming home again. It was obvious something happened to him during his last trip to Dubai, and shortly afterward I was ordered to make the transfer of funds. I think Francisco had only two choices: go to Interpol with his suspicions, or accept a generous offer to compensate him for his loss."

"His loss? We all lost Eliza!" Lucas yelled. "I watched her being taken away rolled in a filthy carpet like a piece of trash! And now I've killed the bastards who did it."

Lucas was flushed and seething with rage. His eyes were piercing Jean-Étienne's cowering face like sharpened spears. His lip was curled in a snarl and his teeth were grinding forward and back, his breath was deep and rapid like a steam engine roaring to life. He was on the verge of exploding in a violent torrent. His hand with the H&K pistol slid from behind his back and hung at his side.

Jean-Étienne visibly aged twenty years in the blink of an eye. What little proud, arrogant swagger that remained of the man vanished, and the waxed leather chair squealed beneath him as he shrank into a ball. The man who had lived in opulence, mingled with kings and queens and never known fear or hunger, was seeing his death on the horizon; and it was fast approaching.

"You didn't get them all!" he cried.

Lucas caught his breath and held it for an instant, letting the pistol slowly rock back and forth in his grasp. "What?"

"You didn't get them all! The rest of the team made it back across the sea to Algiers by the next afternoon," He said.

"How do you know that? How could you possibly know that?" Lucas screamed in the withering old man's face.

"They sent me a message! Farouk said you might be on your way here!" he cried.

Then the horror shone across his face, as he realized he'd emptied his hand. He'd given away what he didn't want Lucas to know. That he was more deeply imbedded in the whole operation, and in constant contact with the evil bastards who planned and orchestrated the kidnappings of little girls, including Eliza.

Then he made one last desperate attempt to salvage his life. "I can give you the names of the others, and where they pick up their money in Algeria and Morocco. I handle all of those payments, I'm the key, can't you see that? I know everyone! I even have to make another deposit for the girls they delivered last week for distribution."

LUCAS DREW A DEEP, slow breath as he stood tall, towering over him. His thoughts were scattered now, dancing around in his skull from here to there. This treachery had more moving parts than he ever considered.

Mallorca, Monaco, Morocco, Algeria; how many more? And then something the old man said stood out in his mind. Distribution. That meant the girls are still alive; they were being kidnapped and delivered alive to someone in North Africa.

The words echoed in his mind, and he fell back into the chair in front of the desk. His expression went blank as he reflected back in time.

The police had grilled him over and over all those years ago in Mallorca, and at the end of it, when they fed Lucas and his father to the dogs of the newspaper wars, they had all convinced him that Eliza was certainly dead; that she had never left the island. His father acted convinced of the same, and that was what drove his mother to end her own life.

But what if it was all a lie? What if she had been delivered alive, to some deviant buyer of human flesh. It was easily possible; Mallorca is only 180 miles across the Mediterranean from the coast of Algiers. The fishing boats run it in one long night's voyage.

And then the next wonderful, and horrifying thought came to his mind; could she still be alive? After so many years, is it possible she might still be alive.

Chapter Twenty-Six

※

Lucas had pulled himself back from the edge just in time. Back from that dark place that delivers the tingling, sensuous wave through the pleasure centers in his brain. The place where he ceased to be human, with human weakness and caring, empathy or pity. The place where the fangs of his primordial self extended to rip the flesh of his enemies and spill their blood. He was hovering in that place, and at the precipice of slaughtering Jean-Étienne Berger like a sacrificial goat, when the epiphany hit him.

It was possible, not likely perhaps, but still possible that Eliza *was* alive. He dared not think any deeper about what she may have gone through, or what condition she might be in now, if in fact she was still alive. But the residue of hope gave him pause. He needed Jean-Étienne to fill in a few more details before he considered killing him.

The next several hours yielded a wealth of information. Names, companies, transactions, and a glimpse into the magnitude of the world that existed behind this world. Banco Baudin, founded by Jean-Étienne's grandfather, was not just a private investment banking company. It was a clearing house for transactions between the two worlds. For three generations, his family had been processing orders for "goods and services" from the power brokers of men who live behind the veil, and ensuring the payments for delivery.

As well, money profited from transactions that fell outside the rules of law that bound the common people, were transitioned through shell companies, filters, to wash away the stains of blood and corruption.

International construction companies, real estate development and management corporations, and oil exploration giants; all operated with the primary purpose of laundering billions and trillions of dollars in blood money. The cleaned money was then placed in landing accounts away from the grubby taxmen of the civilized nations.

Banco Baudin, with a small office nestled on the hillside above Monte Carlo and looking out over the azure blue sea, managed assets and transactions that exceeded the gross national product of some medium-sized countries; and it was just a sliver of the pie.

Jean-Étienne only handled transactions within the Mediterranean and North Africa, and still, it was a considerable business. Throughout the Mediterranean, Africa, and the Middle East were brokers who dealt in the business of human trafficking. Slavery. Their clients ranged from supplying small village brothels, to special orders from princes and kings.

Over decades, they had perfected methods of acquiring, transporting, and delivering kidnapped victims. They had vast networks of contacts and conspirators on payroll at every level. Shipping and customs officials in every major port, local and national law enforcement officers, military officers, judges, religious leaders, and elected politicians.

It was a shell game on the greatest scale ever conceived; an intricate web of misdirection. All working with the singular objective: keep the game hidden from the rest of the world.

As THE FIRST hint of morning sun flickered over the eastern water line, the sea was left cloudy and pale like a deadman's eyes after the night storms had passed. Jean-Étienne's complexion was as pale and grey as the softly rolling sea. It had been a long night. The folds of skin below his eyes drooped with exhaustion, and the crevices of fear that stretched tightly across his forehead hours before, were reduced to flattened pink fault lines. He had no more energy left to whimper or worry; no more tears left to cry for forgiveness.

He knew his life was going to end; he just didn't yet know how or by whose hand. He had given everything to Lucas. Every last detail of an extraordinarily complex organization. A web of evil that reached the corners of the world. The final data was being encrypted into a flash drive as he sat watching the progress bar inching across the screen.

Lucas was looking out the window and across the bay at the city that never slept. Casinos, resorts, clubs, all thriving through night and day with no notice of the sun or moon. He looked down, and just below the terrace of the mansion in the deep water bay was a yacht. A stunning, black-hulled eighty footer, built for high speed blue-water cruising and parties with beautiful women.

"Who's motor yacht is that? The black one in the bay," he asked.

"It's mine." Jean-Étienne replied weakly.

"Beautiful. Looks like she'd handle the open sea very well."

"I wouldn't know, I only use it for social gatherings. It's never left the bay."

As the data load finished he pulled the pin drive from the side of the computer and handed it to Lucas, but never looked up as he spoke, "I'm giving you my soul in this device, Lucas. Is there any hope for my redemption?"

"I have only one more thing I need to know about, Jean-Étienne. Tell me about Eliza."

The weary old man sagged forward over the desk onto his elbows, and buried his face into his hands and spoke through his sweaty palms. "Farouk forced me to tell him where your family would be in the next week. He said he had a special request from an important person. An order for a girl that your sister perfectly matched. I begged him not to do it; your father was a good man and he shouldn't have his daughter taken from him. But you can't say "No" to men like Farouk."

"Was she taken to Algiers?" Lucas asked.

"I believe so. That's where the payments were made to the boat crew. I don't know where she was taken from there. Only Farouk would know. But, Lucas, it would be a fool's errand to try to find her."

Lucas placed the muzzle of the H&K gently against the base of the old man's skull at the tip of the spinal column, and squeezed the trigger.

Chapter Twenty-Seven

✦✦✦

The first beams of sunshine were coming through the windows as Lucas walked down the winding staircase and into the salon. Serge looked liked a mischievous schoolboy sitting in an enormous red tapestry armchair, eating a large wedge of juicy melon and dribbling sticky liquid on the exquisite fabric. He kept his mouth attached to the melon, but looked up at Lucas and raised his eyebrows into an inquisitive arch. Then he slurped and gulped a bite and asked, "How did your chat with the banker go?"

"Very profitable, in more ways than one."

"Excellent! While you were upstairs, I located the security monitoring system in the basement and pulled all of the discs. The old man was too paranoid to have it monitored remotely; I guess he didn't want anyone to hack in and spy on his activities here at the house."

"Nice work."

Avi was asleep on the brown leather sofa, curled into a ball with her arms wrapped tightly around her knees, and her black hair shielding her swollen eyes and bruised face from the morning light. Lucas stopped at the bottom step of the stairs and contemplated this woman that he suddenly felt drawn to.

She had a copper-colored Spanish shawl wrapped around her upper body to keep her warm, but Berger's men had nearly stripped her. Her long, bare legs were coiled against the front of her, and she no longer held the bearing of the invincible woman he had met in the office. She was fully defensive, shielding herself from physical and emotional harm, like a young girl; transporting her mind into another reality to block the one where her body lingered.

"How is she?" Lucas asked.

"She hasn't said a word since she came down the stairs last night. She's been on the sofa just like that. I think she's finally asleep, but she was squirming around for a while and she kept swiping at her skin like she had spiders crawling over her. The shawl was hanging on the wall and I pulled it down for her. I offered to find her a blanket or something, but she wouldn't answer me."

Lucas felt the electric tingle of the cell phone vibrating in his front pocket; the phone Diggs had given him. He walked through into the living and dining area of the house, stood by the window that looked out over the bay and answered it, "Good news about the meeting?"

"Our sources tell us the meeting is in three days in Palma. Are you interested in a second interview?"

"Absolutely."

"How did your chat with Berger go?"

"I have a lot more information than I had before. Ever heard of a guy named Farouk Kateb?"

"Yes. Farouk will be the at the head of the table in Mallorca. We aren't sure where he is originally from, but somehow he landed an ambassadorship post with the Algerian government. He travels with a full security team everywhere he goes, and he operates with total diplomatic immunity."

"He's not immune from me," Lucas said.

"You need to be here within the next thirty hours, but since your last visit to the island the authorities might be screening for someone of your description at the airport. You'll have to find another way to arrive. I don't think they know who killed the Moroccans, but it would be safer to avoid the police gauntlet."

Lucas stared out over the flat water as the morning tide was just beginning to turn in, and the gentle pitch of the sea made the big black yacht yaw against her anchor. "I have another option, I'll make it. I'm going to my family villa in Port d'Andratx first, and I'll call you when I arrive."

"I know where your villa is, I'll be expecting to hear from you."

"Should I even ask how you already know that?"

"Unimportant details at the moment, Lucas. Stay focused. I'll be waiting for your call."

LUCAS TURNED TO SERGE, "How would you feel about coming to Mallorca with me?"

"Another hunting party?"

"A big party."

Serge jumped up from the red chair and flung the melon rind across the floor, "I'm in. Last night was the most fun I've had in years."

Lucas looked out the window and down at the motor-yacht, "Let's take a boat ride. She looks fast, eh. What do you think, twenty knots?"

Serge walked to the window and saw the black beauty tugging against the bow line, "Ha! That's an AB100 super yacht. She'll probably cruise at forty knots with flat water. I'll check with the weather service about sea conditions, but if we have fair weather, we can make Mallorca in under 12 hours in that rocket. Faster than standing in line at the airport and flying through Barcelona or Rome."

"Retrieve the rest of the gear from the car, and

then burn it. I just came into some cash, so I'll buy you a new one if we make it off Mallorca in one piece."

"TAKE ME WITH YOU, LUCAS," Avi said.

He looked up and saw her standing in the entry hall. Her silky hair pulled forward and covering her blouse, torn open from the top with only two of the lower buttons remaining to hold it closed over her midsection, and the long tails hanging down over her hips and ivory-colored lace panties. She walked toward him, and his eyes were drawn to her toenails, painted an iridescent pink, as her bare feet stuck and squeaked over the freshly waxed floors; then his gaze trailed up the impossibly long, tanned legs as they propelled her forward.

He expected to feel the sickening need to turn away from her, as he had with every woman before, but it never came. He was warmly transfixed by the sight of her.

"Avi, this won't be safe for you, and I might be on the wanted-list in Mallorca already."

"I can't stay here, Lucas. These men aren't the only ones working for Jean-Étienne, and when they find out he's dead they'll hunt me down. I have no job, no money, no home I can go back to. Please, if you don't take me, I'm dead."

Lucas stood looking into her eyes, and without

turning away, said to Serge, "I'll find a motor launch to get us out to the yacht, and we'll meet you at the dock in two hours."

Chapter Twenty-Eight

❧

The man had been sitting at a small, ornately decorated ceramic table on the terrace for most of the morning. His black hair was neatly cropped and combed, his dark beard had a precisely maintained three day stubble, and his tailored Armani suit fit perfectly, even as he sat patiently in one place for hours.

His name was Abd al-Rahman, meaning, *Servant of the Compassionate One*, which was hardly fitting in this particular case.

Rising from the lower class, he had served with great distinction in the Saudi military and special intelligence corp; and when his commander moved into civilian life with a private security firm, he followed. Now, eight years later, he was the eyes and ears in the field, the finger tips of the chess master, moving pieces in the grand game. He was also a ruthless assassin.

On the table in front of him was a cup of herbal tea, and implements of his trade; a pair of 20X binoculars, a moleskin notepad and silver pen, and an encrypted cell phone. He had been sitting on this terrace alone every morning and afternoon for the last two days, only interrupting his vigil to make or receive a few calls. He had rented out the entire villa with a spectacular view of the sea and the villas below on the far side of the bay, for the sum of ten-thousand euros per day, to ensure complete privacy for his work.

He was a conductor of sorts, planning and orchestrating events in melodious sequence. He was assisted by a team of highly-trained operatives who hovered closer to the action and relayed information, and he was about to make his last report to his patron before departing.

He looked through the binoculars at the yacht that was underway, cruising at quarter throttles in a southerly heading into the blue horizonless water, then he lay the optics on the table, brought the fine china cup of tea to his lips for a sip, and picked up his cell phone and dialed #1 on speed dial.

"I have news, put me through to him," he said.

The voice of the personal bodyguard who answered the phone responded, "At once."

Abd-al Rahman could hear the light clicking of hard rubber shoes moving over polished marble floors, and then muffled for several steps as they passed over elegant Persian carpets. He subconsciously counted the footfalls and scribed a mental map from the number of steps through the room, and then the twisting sound of the shoe sole as the man pivoted at the bottom of the staircase.

He could tell precisely how tall the bodyguard was by the timing of his climb up the winding stairs, as he effortlessly scaled every other step of thirty-seven to the top. His pace had slowed by half a second per step on the last four. *Too much time sitting on his ass in the limo; his conditioning is weak,* Abd al-Rahman thought.

"Tell me," came the voice on the phone.

FAROUK KATEB WAS NOT a man who thought of patience as a virtue. He was direct, he was demanding, and he took whatever he wanted, when he wanted it. His true nationality was unknown, although some suspected he may have been born in Palestine, and fled across the border into Egypt as a boy. It was known that he had strong sympathies for the Palestinian people, and despised the Israelis.

By his teen years he was working in the criminal underworld of Algiers, and at the age of twenty-seven he assassinated his boss and seized control of a regional network that specialized in smuggling heroin from Afghanistan, across the desert by way of camels, and then delivering it in small fishing boats across the Mediterranean Sea into Spain.

Ten years later, his business was cross-pollinated with human trafficking, and then front-companies like fishing vessel consortiums to conceal the movement of goods, and launder the proceeds through legally established enterprises. He was so successful at it, that he soon became a partner of sorts in several businesses that operated entirely as funding arms for Hezbollah.

He maintained offices in Beirut, Cairo, and Algiers. He was known as a man who could move anything to anywhere, and fulfill extraordinary requests; for the right price.

He became a very wealthy and powerful man in his adopted country, and because of his ability to manage the flow of commerce outside the law, hide assets, and throw lavish parties with beautiful women, he soon became a close personal acquaintance of the Prime Minister of Algeria. In 2012 he was appointed as the first Algerian Ambassador to Spain.

"Your Excellency, he proved himself to be very efficient. He eliminated all of the security detail, and then spent the entire night interrogating Monsieur Berger. He ended the interrogation at 6:40 this morning, left the residence promptly, and is now underway aboard Berger's yacht. I believe he is heading to Mallorca. Avigail has joined him for the voyage."

"Do you have recordings of the interrogation?"

"Yes, Your Excellency. I monitored the entire evening's events, and have clear transcripts. Jean-Étienne gave him everything on the current organization in Africa and Europe. He also gave Lucas access to the accounts of Francisco Martell, in their entirety. Something we had not anticipated," he said.

"That's unfortunate, but it's an insignificant matter. He won't have time to enjoy it," the voice answered. Then he added, "As for the information he has on the organization, it will all be irrelevant very soon."

"Shall we eliminate him from the game board, or keep him in play, Your Excellency?"

Farouk thought for a moment before answering, "Let him arrive safely in Mallorca, his corpse might prove more useful at the party."

Chapter Twenty-Nine

THE MEDITERRANEAN SEA

The AB100 yacht was kept fully loaded for extended parties and cruising. It had three sleeping cabins, a fully stocked galley, and a maintenance shop below deck; an open air party deck, an elegantly appointed salon, and a forward master suite on the first level. The second and third levels had an integrated office complex, full bridge with oceanic navigation, communications center, and radar.

At one-hundred feet in length, it was big enough to be a luxurious cruiser, but light enough to be built for speed. It was powered by three nineteen-hundred horsepower turbo diesel Volvo Marine engines. Each engine had three individual water-jet drives for thrust and maneuvering.

Serge fired the monster engines to life at 9:45 a.m., and let them idle to warm up. Then, he switched on the navigation system and plotted in the GPS coordinates for the horseshoe bay at Port d'Andratx on the western shore of Mallorca. The big AB100 could nearly navigate herself on autopilot in fair weather, requesting only minor throttle input and steering in rougher water, but this morning the weather was fair and the Mediterranean was calm.

At exactly 10:00, he grasped the three throttle levers together in his right hand and drove them forward, and the boat shuddered as the engines roared below decks and pushed her sharp bow through the incoming tide. A moment later they felt her lift her head and settle up high in the water, and the speedometer raced to 43 knots.

Lucas nodded and smiled, "Keep her at this speed as long as the weather holds, and we'll be drinking whiskey in my villa before midnight. I need to sleep for a few hours, then I'll come up and relieve you."

"Where's the woman," Serge asked.

"I saw her go into one of the cabins below deck an hour ago. I'm going to the master cabin. Leave her alone, she's had people trying to kill her and torturing her for the last two days."

Lucas walked down the tight spiral steel stairs to the main level, and down the narrow passageway to the master cabin. The floor of the hall was polished teak, and the walls were painted in a non-reflective green colored background, with small recessed lighting on the edges and in the ceiling. Along the walls were gold-framed reproductions of famous artworks that matched the decor of the mansion on the cliff. The old banker was fond of the classical painters. Lucas opened the dark mahogany door to the suite and stepped into the dimly lit cabin. His senses told him instantly that he was not alone.

The cabin shades were shuttered tight, so he couldn't see her in the darkness. Nor could he hear her, because she remained as still and quiet as a ghost. But he could smell her. The intoxicating scent of a freshly bathed woman's flesh. The clean, sweet odor had left a lingering trail as she passed through the door and into the room. He detected the fruity aroma of shampoo in her hair, a crisp tart smell like *pelom blanco* nectarines.

He stood frozen, trying to decide whether to quietly retreat, or feign ignorance and turn on the lights in the cabin. He desperately wanted to see her, but he wasn't sure he could fake his surprise if he startled her. He slowly turned and reached for the door handle, and then she spoke, "I don't want to be alone, Lucas. Please, stay with me."

His eyes were adjusting quickly to the lack of light, dilating from an instant flood of adrenaline. He could make out the curve of her hips under a dark silk sheet, sloping down to her narrow waist. She was lying on her side, facing the center of the large king-sized bed with the cover pulled up under her arm, and her hair wet-braided into a long rope that stretched out over the pillow behind her.

"Please, Lucas. I'm so afraid right now; it would make me feel safe if you just lie here with me while I try to sleep."

It was the moment he had always feared in his conscious mind. The moment that fate would force him into the close proximity of a beautiful woman. So close that the urges he tried hard to suppress, those urges that flooded him with shame and guilt, would break free. He thought of it as the darkness that takes a man's soul and casts it to the flames. A monster that, once loose, can never again be contained.

But in his dreams, the ones that came in the deepest levels of sleep, he begged the heavens for this day to arrive. The day when he could confront the demons of his past, and this was his chance. She needed him to be near, and he needed to save her from her fears.

"I ... my clothes are covered with filth and blood," he said.

"Take them off and come next to me, it's alright," she said.

He bent over and unstrapped his boots, then pulled them off and pushed them to the wall. He pulled his soiled black shirt up over his head and lay it over the boots, unbuckled his belt and let his pants fall to his ankles and stepped out of them. It was the first of many terrifying steps he was about to take, as he stood bare except for his Legion-issued shorts, for the first time in the sight of a woman.

Avi could see him in the shadows. He was tall and lean, wide shoulders and narrow hips. She saw the contour of his muscles clearly in the gray light, a chiseled stone core, and filaments that flexed and moved through his shoulders and arms as he nervously drew his hands in front and clasped them together.

She could vaguely see the artwork of ink that covered his right arm; watch-words of honor and bravery, places he'd fought and killed, and depictions of spirits that brought him strength.

She gestured with her hand for him to come to her, and lifted the corner of the sheet for him. His throat bound up and felt like he was about to swallow his own tongue as he moved to the bed, and sat on the edge.

She held the sheet up for him to come under, and even though he couldn't quite see her body, her overwhelming aura was even more powerful as it escaped from under the cover. He slid quickly beneath it and lay flat on his back, hands over his stomach, and eyes staring into the dark ceiling. The sheets were cool against his skin, and his body shivered.

"You're trembling," she said.

Lucas didn't respond.

Avi moved close to him, laid her soft cheek neatly over the crease between his bicep and his chest, and wrapped her arm around him. He could feel the heat of her breasts pressed against his ribs, and her smooth belly molding along the outline of his hip and thigh.

She pressed closer still, and raised her knee over his leg to clutch him tighter as though her life depended on holding him there. He felt the sensation of stinging needles everywhere her warm skin touched his, and he didn't want it to end. He stayed completely motionless, reveling in his first sensual embrace.

In a short time, he felt Avi's breath slowing into a deep rhythm, and knew she had fallen fast asleep. He thought back to what Louisa had said to him, and now he understood. Yes, passion is madness; but it is not evil.

His own exhaustion finally overtook him, and he drifted off to sleep.

THE MOVEMENT WOKE HIM. The engines winding down and the big yacht rolling forward as she sunk deeper into the water and slowed. Avi was still lying exactly as she had been; he slid quietly out from under, and held her head until he tucked the pillow under it. He pulled his clothes back on and left the room, making his way up to the bridge to see what had happened.

"Why are we slowing down. Is something wrong?" he said, as he climbed the stairs into the bridge.

"Nothing wrong, Sleepy. We're one mile off the coast of Port d'Andratx."

"What? That's not possible. I just went to sleep a few minutes ago."

"Lucas, see how dark it is outside? It's 9:47 p.m. You've been asleep for almost eleven hours. I came in to check on you five hours ago, but you looked pretty comfortable. No way I was going to interrupt that. So I just caught a cat-nap up here on the bridge. The self-navigation was working great and the sea was flat; no big deal."

"I can't remember sleeping like that since I was a kid." Lucas said.

He looked ahead through the windshield and could see a few scattered lights of houses on the hillside above the bay, and got his bearings. "Take her in to about three-hundred meters and set anchor. We'll go ashore on the skiff and walk up to the villa."

Chapter Thirty

MALLORCA

They came ashore on the skiff at midnight, killing the small outboard engine as it drew near the shore, and coasting in on the tide. The sugary sand of the beach squeaked as the bow dug in and the boat slid to a stop; Lucas jumped out with his pant legs rolled up and his bare feet landed with a squishy plop. The wet sand was cool and soothing in the thick summer air. It felt like home.

He pulled the heavy block anchor and rope from the bow, dragged the boat another three feet onto the beach, and set the anchor into the ground above the waterline.

Lucas groped in the dark for the hidden key when they arrived up the hill at the front door to his villa, and found it precisely as before. They came in, turned on the lights, and each attended to a different task.

Serge went from room to room with his gun forward, to make sure the house was clear.

Avi went to the kitchen and located the coffee and started brewing a fresh pot.

Lucas pulled out the cell phone that Diggs had given him and made the call, "We're at my villa in Port d'Andratx."

"Yes, I know. I'll be there in a few hours and we can go over the meeting details and inventory supplies. We'll have one day to scout the locations."

"I would ask how you knew we'd already arrived, but I realize it's an unimportant detail."

"You're learning, that's a good sign. You might actually survive this."

DIGGS APPEARED at the front door at precisely 5:00. "Ready to get to work? We have a lot of ground to cover."

Lucas introduced Serge, "Diggs, this is my friend, Serge. He was the best armorer in the Legion and a very proficient sniper. He's saved my ass more than a few times."

Diggs nodded at Serge, but didn't offer his hand, "I'm aware of his talents."

Lucas turned toward the kitchen where Avi was sitting at the small round table, warming her hands around a mug of steaming coffee, "This is…"

Diggs interrupted, "Michele, or would you prefer, Avigail."

Avi looked surprised, but tried to remain calm, "Avigail is fine."

Lucas tried to defuse the tension, "He does this. He just knows things."

"Lucas, we have a lot to cover. Where are we working?" Diggs said.

Lucas, Diggs, and Serge spent the morning reviewing the latest intel on the meeting. The best information they had suggested that three different men involved in the trafficking and smuggling trade were due to arrive at Palma International Airport the next day, at various times. Where they were staying was unknown, only that the meeting was set for late afternoon on a yacht in the harbor. The harbor stretched out into the sea, directly in front the La Seu Cathedral, the most historic and public location on the island.

Diggs gave them some background, "The men coming in represent the largest distribution and logistics channel for heroin, hashish, and human trafficking in the Middle East, Africa, and Northern Europe.

Bharath Al-Maadeed from Qatar; Pieter van de Rud from Belgium; and Frederik Renier from Capetown. They've all formed something of a working alliance over the past eight years with Farouk Kateb. Farouk's diplomatic position gives them all access to information and banking connections to clean their money and tuck it safely away in remote parts of the world.

Together, they control ninety percent of the slave trade on two continents, sixty percent of the opium distribution into Europe and Scandinavia, and most of the poaching trade from central Africa that's destined to Far East clientele.

Conservatively speaking, about two-hundred billion dollars per year in revenue. The word on the wire is that Farouk is entertaining the idea of working with arms dealers as well, because his fundraising connections with Hezbollah are directing him to get into the business. The three others are concerned about branching out into work that might draw the scrutiny of Allied agencies, which the gun trade certainly would."

Serge asked, "Could we hit them in transit, before they get into the city center?"

"That's an option. Normally when these men meet, the three leave their own security teams at the airport, and Farouk provides a pair of diplomatic limousines. Two passengers ride in each, with two of Farouk's security team, and local police escorts to their meeting place. Farouk always rides in the first car; he likes to be at the head of the line."

"Do you know if the limousines are customized bulletproof vehicles?" Serge asked.

"I'm sure they are," Diggs said.

"I brought along some armor-piercing incendiary rounds for my rifle. If you can get me the exact make and model, and better yet, which company did the armoring, then I'll know exactly where the fuel tanks are, and I can place shots that will turn the cars into a fireball. We can do this on a lonely stretch of road and get them all in three seconds without a scratch."

"I need Farouk alive," Lucas said. "There are things I need to know that only he can tell me. We can't risk killing him with the others."

"What? That's just stupid, Lucas," Serge retorted.

"Stupid or not, that's the way it is."

"How are we going to kill three and capture one?" Serge said.

"Our only chance is to hit them on the yacht. We'll do it the same way we hit Berger's mansion; you shooting from above, and Diggs and I will board the boat."

Diggs stood up and stretched his back, "Lucas, let's get some air."

They walked out through the French doors onto the stone terrace that looked out over the bay. Diggs stood by the balustrade and saw the big black motor yacht moored outside the breakwater, "The banker's boat?" he asked.

"Yes. Nice ride, really fast for a motor yacht."

"Lucas, I know you are intent on taking Farouk Kateb alive, and I know why you want him. But if we come aboard that yacht and have to carefully monitor every shot for fear of killing the wrong man, it puts us at a distinct disadvantage. Everyone on that yacht needs to be put down as quickly as possible."

Then Diggs shifted the subject, "Lucas, how much do you know about the girl, Avigail?"

"She told me she was from Israel, but grew up in Algeria. I know she was working for Berger at the time my sister was kidnapped, and she's seen the man who did it. She knows what Farouk Kateb looks like. And I know she tried to help me in Monte Carlo, and almost got killed for her trouble."

"If we all make it out of this tomorrow, we'll be moving fast to get off this island. You might never be able to come back here again. If you care about her, my suggestion is you put her on a plane to somewhere else. Today," Diggs said.

Lucas turned and looked back into the house, and could see Avi, still sitting at the table and looking back at him. There was something about her, something that disarmed him and comforted him. "I'll talk to her about it," he said.

"Avi, I think it might be best if you leave Mallorca today. I can wire money to you, I have plenty so you don't need to worry about that. You could fly out this afternoon and go anywhere you want to go. When this is all over, I'll come to you," Lucas said.

She looked wounded, and panicked, "I don't want to leave, Lucas. Please don't make me. The only place I feel safe is right here with you."

"That's the point, Avi. I can't keep you safe here. What we're going to do tomorrow … I don't know how it's going to end. It would make me feel better if I knew you were someplace safe before it all went down."

She held her head down and shielded her face from him, then looked up into his eyes, "Let me stay tonight. Just one night, and I'll fly wherever you tell me to go, first thing in the morning. Just tonight, please," she begged.

Then she reached over the table with both hands and held his wrists. Her hands looked so delicate, her wrists and arms were slender and soft. She was wearing a beautifully jeweled bracelet; silver with engraved beads and rounded gemstones. He reached over and touched it gently with his thumb, "That's a beautiful bracelet," he said.

"It belonged to my mother. It's the only thing I have of her, and I never take it off."

He looked back into her entrancing gray-green eyes, "Alright. I'm going to book you on the 6:00 a.m. flight to Rome. We'll be leaving early, and I'll take you to the airport first."

LATER THAT NIGHT, Lucas came down the long narrow hallway, and as he passed the door to his parents' room, where Avi was sleeping, he heard the door open and turned to see her standing just inside the threshold. The lights were off in the room and it was dark, but the faint light from the hall, a weak incandescent yellow on its own, fell over her bare body and transformed to a warm, fleshy tone.

Her hair had been brushed back to a luster that gleamed even in the weak light, and it draped over her shoulders, around her breasts, and tapered to her hips. She appeared as an irresistible specter, and without uttering a word she beckoned him to come to her arms.

Lucas started to speak, "Avi … I," but she reached up and stopped him with the lightest touch of her finger to his lips. She took his hand, and pulled him into the darkness.

He stood frozen in the void, unable to see her. He flinched when her hands touched his chest; she found the top button of his shirt and slipped it back through the opening, and then fluidly moved downward to undo them all. She took the shirt and spread it open and around his shoulders and down, and he lifted his arms free as it drifted to the floor.

As her fingertips moved over the waist of his pants and unsnapped the button, she felt the same trembling in his core that she felt when he was lying on the bed next to her on the yacht. Many men had trembled in her hands before, but never like this. This wasn't a trembling response of anticipation, or pleasure; it was the response of man who was facing the unknown. She wondered how it could be.

She loosened his pants and pulled them to the floor together with his shorts, and he stepped out of them as bare as he'd first come into the world. She pressed herself against him, and he could feel the searing heat of her body; then she pulled away and took his hands in hers and led him through the darkness to the bed. She could feel the slightest hesitation as she pulled him forward, and the fire growing inside him.

THE STORY that Avigail had shared with Lucas in Monte Carlo, about her early life and how she came to be there, was not entirely accurate. In fact, very little resembled the truth. She was born in Tel Aviv to an Israeli mother and an Algerian father, that much was true.

But her father was not a benevolent man, nor a loving husband. He beat his wife until her family threatened to kill him. And when it became apparent that they were going to have him deported, he took his two daughters and fled.

He took the girls with the sole intention of wounding his wife and her family, and perhaps demanding a sizable ransom, but not long after arriving in Algeria he realized the two girls could bring a handsome price right there in Algiers. At the ages of eight and six they were sold into slavery by their own father.

Avi's life was an unending tale of misery and abuse until she reached her fourteenth birthday. Two things happened in that year. First, she began to rapidly mature, and it was evident to everyone who saw her that her beauty could be extraordinary if she was allowed to live in a healthier environment.

And second, she caught the eye of a powerful and well connected man, Farouk Kateb. Farouk acquired her, and groomed her for a very specific purpose. He hired private tutors to educate her; health and nutritional professionals to heal her and shape her to perfection; and lastly, a mentor in the art of sexual pleasure.

When she performed well and impressed her teachers, Farouk treated her with kindness and affection. But if she failed or refused any of their directives, his cruelty knew no bounds. She gradually learned to do only those things that pleased him. She would do his bidding, no matter what he asked of her. Farouk was a tyrant, but he also became the closest thing to a father that she had any hopes of having in this life.

As SHE PULLED him onto the bed, Avi knew immediately that Lucas was not like any of the men she had been forced into bed with in all the years before. All of them were older, ugly men. They were domineering and rough, some violent; and they regarded her like a disposable object.

But from the moment they fell together across the soft cotton sheets, Lucas was gentle. He had moved past his fear of making love to a woman, and now his only fear was of somehow hurting her.

He touched her, and caressed her as he might something of incredible value; something fragile and fleeting that would crumble under the weight of his clumsy hands. He used the soft flesh on the back of his hand to stroke her skin, rather than touch her with his cracked and calloused fingers, unhurriedly passing over her with an almost imperceptible feel, like the downy feather of a dove.

He held his full weight above her, and she clasped his face in her hands and guided his lips to hers. They were moist and swollen; she kissed him delicately at first, then more passionately as she felt his lips swelling with hers. Her tongue parted the way and nimbly probed for the tip of his, and teased it with a circular touch.

He was bewildered by the fire that burned through him. Every nerve in his body seemed to be racing desperately to the places where his flesh met hers, to reach through the barrier that kept their souls apart.

She released his lips and directed them to the soft base of her neck, and as he worked his way further down, her body rose to greet him. A whimper rushed from her lungs as he made an unexpected discovery. When she was ready for him, she pulled him tightly to her and gripped him with her firm thighs; he felt the moist warmth of her body envelope him, and for a while, the world around them disappeared.

THE MOONLIGHT WAS BREACHING the shades, and the room was a monotone canvas. Avi watched him as he slept. Even in this moment of rest after passion, she could see the pain and anger that lingered in him. The corners of his eyes would clench, the lines across his forehead deepened. He was thinking about Farouk. He was thinking about his sister, and watching helplessly as she was stolen from him.

The evil that befell Lucas' family had destroyed them, and set Lucas on the path that took him through the deserts of Africa; the path of a killer. And now that path might lead him to his death. She had a hand in that evil. Whether willing or not, there was no denying it; she was part of the treachery.

And as she watched, she knew that her own life had been shaped by the same evil. She was exactly what Farouk had made her. Her only means of surviving all these years was to embrace that evil, and be whatever her master wanted her to be.

Lucas flinched and jerked in his sleep, and his face grimaced against a phantom enemy. She laid her hand on his shoulder, and he relaxed. "This is the only man who has ever defended me. He barely knows me, but I think he would die for me," she whispered to herself in the gray light.

"This is a man I could love ..."

Chapter Thirty-One
PALMA, MALLORCA

Before sunrise, they were driving through town in a silver rental van. As they came in on the main highway, Ma-1 and passed the La Seu Cathedral, the van slowed to a rolling stop and Serge stepped out on the curb and instantly into a trot down the sidewalk.

His mission was to enter the cathedral, find his way up to the highest window of the northwest bell tower, and set up a shooting position.

The van continued on for another five minutes to the International Airport, and stopped in front of Departures. Lucas turned in his seat and looked at Avi, "Take the 6:00 flight to Rome, and check into the Palazzo Montemartini Hotel. I paid for the room last night, online. When this is all over and I know it's safe for me to come, I'll join you there."

Avi looked at him and opened her mouth to

speak, but pulled the words back. She kissed her own fingertips, then reached forward and touched them to his; then she drew open the side door of the van and stepped out. She turned back to Lucas, "I'm so sorry all of this happened to your family, Lucas. I'm sorry for everything …" Then she reached for the door.

The instant she closed the door behind her, Diggs accelerated away from the curb and looped back onto the highway. "Farouk and the others aren't suppose to arrive at the harbor before midday, but we'll need to be in position long before then."

The intel that Diggs had placed the group of Farouk Kateb, Bharath Al-Maadeed, Pieter van de Rud, and Frederik Renier arriving together at the harbor and meeting on a yacht that was owned by a Lebanese businessman.

The yacht remained moored at the very end of the dock year-round, and was used for entertaining clients and private gatherings. It came with its own two-man security detail and was swept daily for listening devices. It was a perfect neutral ground for meetings among thieves and criminals.

Serge was to set up a shooting post in the only available high ground in Palma with a view of the harbor, the bell tower in the historic La Seu Cathedral. From the arched opening under the bell, he had a direct line of sight down the long dock that moored the luxury yachts of Mallorca.

The yacht that Farouk and the others were using for their gathering was exactly 857 meters from the northwest tower, just under half a mile. It was well within the reach of both the rifle, and Serge's shooting ability, as long as the afternoon winds didn't pick up.

Diggs took Lucas back to Port d'Andratx, where he would take the skiff from the big black racing yacht "borrowed" from Jean-Étienne Berger, and cruise his way leisurely back along the coast toward the Palma harbor.

Skiffs and motor launches were a regular sight among the larger vessels, shuttling wealthy patrons to and fro, delivering food, wine, supplies to the galley crews, and tending to exterior maintenance on the big boats.

With a hat, sunglasses, shorts, and a shirtless tanned physique, Lucas would blend in perfectly. He would have been spotted a mile away if he tried to walk straight down the dock, but masquerading as a harbor worker, he was invisible.

His mission was to work his way alongside the meeting yacht, climb aboard without being detected, and sweep from the bridge down through the three levels; killing anyone who came across his path with the silenced H&K pistol. Every person onboard was to be considered a hostile.

Diggs was a ghost. No one knew what he looked like, and to the best of his knowledge, that he even existed. He could walk down the length of the dock admiring the yachts and not raise a hint of alarm.

He would wait for confirmation that Lucas had entered and was in position, and he would then step directly onto the rear deck and begin killing everyone from the lower deck and working upward.

If any unaccounted for guards came into view of Serge's rifle, he would strike them down with a muffled thunderbolt from his cathedral cloud.

Each of the three was wearing micro earpiece units, which were borrowed from the U.S. National Reconnaissance Office, and technically, didn't exist. They nestled deep into the ear canal where they couldn't be detected, and they picked up vibrations from the temporal bone that transmitted speech as well as receiving incoming communication.

All three could hear and speak to each other with nothing more than a whisper, to coordinate their assault on the yacht. Range was the only drawback to the devices, as they had to be within a mile or less to clearly receive and send transmissions.

Lucas took his time on the journey to Palma, admiring the rugged coastline and beautiful boats, and even more beautiful women. He couldn't arrive too early because they wanted the group to settle down and get comfortable, and the guards to relax. Afternoon was perfect, as the heat was intense and the guards and guests would be inside the air-conditioned interior of the yacht and not out on the sundeck.

Serge had easily snuck into the cathedral through an open window in one of the administrative offices, found a maintenance closet with cleaning supplies and dirty gray coveralls, and posed as a janitor. He pushed a mop-bucket through the center of the grand church and up to the tower stairwell without notice, carrying his small daypack with a disassembled sniper rifle over his shoulder.

By 9:00 he was lying out on a cloth mat with his rifle scope trained on the rear deck of the yacht, and all of his shooting formulas calculated on a small notepad next to a box with ten, tall brass cartridges standing at the ready.

He ate a candy bar at 10:00, then took a nap until 11:00. At precisely 12:45, he could hear the motorcade coming down Ma-1; two Mallorca motorcycle cops leading two black Mercedes S550 armored limos.

They turned into the harbor entrance. The motorcycle cops stopped their bikes and blocked traffic in and out, allowing the cars unfettered access to drive the length of the harbor dock and deliver their passengers directly in front of the last yacht.

The driver of the first car exited and quickly took up station to open the rear doors. Farouk Kateb stepped out first, as expected, and walked quickly to the ramp. Behind him in the first limousine came the Belgian, Pieter van de Rud.

The driver of the second car then pulled forward, and followed the same pattern. The South African and Arab exited the vehicle and made their way swiftly to the boat ramp, glancing nervously around them as if paranoia was a constant companion.

Then Serge noticed the second driver hesitate, rather than closing the rear door, as if someone else was still in the car.

He saw the glint coming off the polished black heel that reached out from the rear seat, and the slender, bronzed leg that followed it. It planted on the deck and a delicate hand reached out for assistance, which the driver dutifully obeyed by offering his elbow for support.

The driver pulled the woman up from the car, and stepped back with a courteous bow, and she stood tall and shook her thick black hair loose. She turned casually and gave a brief glance in the direction of the La Seu Cathedral, and then turned and boarded the yacht behind the four men. It was Avigail.

Serge's mouth fell open. He couldn't quite process what he'd just seen. "We dropped her off at the airport hours ago, how did she get here? *Why* is she here?" he said to himself. Then it hit him; she wasn't the helpless woman she feigned when she begged Lucas to bring her with him to Mallorca. She was here for a reason. She was here working for him. For Farouk.

Holy shit, our op is blown, he thought to himself. *She's told them everything!*

He was about to communicate his warning to Lucas and Diggs, when he heard an ancient wooden floorboard creak behind him. He rolled over on his side just in time to see it coming. A dark skinned man, a blur of movement, and a flashing blade.

Chapter Thirty-Two

ᨌᨛᨛᨛᨛ

Lucas powered himself up the rope hand-over-hand until he reached the gunwale of the first deck. He grabbed it with his left hand, let go of the rope and pulled his H&K pistol with the silencer out with his right.

Doing a one-armed pull-up, he peered over the rail with the gun in front, and when he was sure it was clear, he swung his leg up, hooked a heel over the gunwale and rolled over onto the deck.

He crouched low and crept around the outside catwalk, then took the stairs up to the bridge and looked in through the side glass. It was empty, so he entered there and took the inside spiral stairs down to the next level, sweeping the gun from side to side with his vision trained on the shadows and doorways. The top two levels of the giant yacht were both completely devoid of life.

He paused next to one of the air-conditioning vents that would have channels flowing from level to level, and listened intently for any sounds from other parts of the vessel, but heard nothing.

As he came down the stairs into the main salon of the boat, he walked into the aftermath of a violent crime scene.

He spoke in a deep tone for the earpiece transmitter to pick up the sound of his voice, "Diggs, we've got a situation. Someone beat us to the punch. I've got three bodies on board, all cut to ribbons. Looks like someone hacked them up with a sword."

Diggs' voice crackled in his earpiece, "Lucas get out of there now, it's…" was all he heard before a crashing blow came across the back of his head. He saw brilliant flashes of red light; the floor coming up to meet his face; then nothing.

DIGGS HAD BEEN SLOWLY WALKING along the moorings, pausing occasionally to take a photograph of a particularly beautiful yacht. He arrived at 1:30, near the harbor by way of a local taxi, bought a map and spent a few minutes chatting with the young girl at the Tourism office. Then he casually lingered in front of the cathedral, and took some photographs of the magnificent building before walking across the main road to the harbor.

He was nearing the end of the dock and listening intently when he heard Lucas' breathing get heavy and raspy for a moment as he climbed up the rope and over the gunwale. Ninety seconds later, he heard the message about the bodies and tried to warn Lucas, but the signal went dead.

He tried to communicate with Serge; no response. Either both earpiece transmitters had mysteriously failed at the same time, or both of them were out of commission. He was flying blind, and alone, in the fight.

Lucas' hearing drifted back first. A high-pitched ringing in his right ear that slowly settled into static white-noise. He could hear foot steps lightly padding across the teak flooring, and then a voice, speaking in Arabic, "Wake up my friend. You have a decision to make."

Lucas struggled to open his eyes but they were heavy as lead. He strained and blinked and pulled them open, seeing only a blurry landscape at first, and then a bright light. As it came into focus, he found he was tied to a dark mahogany dining chair, facing the glass doors that opened to the lower party deck, and the afternoon sun was beating down on him. He squinted against the glare and tried to see who was speaking to him.

"I'm here," said the voice. The tall, slender man stepped out in front of him and blocked the sun from his eyes. Two more men, both wearing tailored black suits, and armed with MP7 machine guns were positioned on opposite sides of the glass doors.

"It would be polite for me to introduce myself, as you will shortly be sent to whatever god you pray to, and I will be the one who assists you on that journey. My name is Abd al-Rahman."

Lucas didn't answer, his neck hurt like hell and he struggled to raise his head to look into the man's eyes.

"Did you not understand me? Perhaps I should speak in your native tongue," he said, and he repeated himself in Spanish.

Then he said, "You are going to die, Señor Martell. But how you die will be entirely your choice. If you cooperate with me, I will end your life humanely. If you do not, it will be slow and quite excruciating."

Lucas answered in Arabic, "What do you want from me?"

Abd al-Rahman looked surprised, and smiled. "You are an educated man. Excellent. I require only two things from you. First, the whereabouts of the American agent you are working for. The man from the Fairhope Group. We have already located your associate in the tower at the cathedral and eliminated him with the assistance of Avigail. But the old man was not where she said he would be."

Lucas felt his heart slump into the pit of his stomach. He tried not to show it on his face, but his entire world had just crashed down around him, again. It was the same life-ending feeling as he had lying in the gravel after being pummeled by the Moroccan, and watching them drive away with Eliza.

"Ah, that stings doesn't it? She's quite a beauty, and I can imagine that you were very taken with her. Most men are," al-Rahman said.

"Where is she?" Lucas said.

"The little dove came back to us this morning, and now she's with her master, Farouk. She flies for a time like she's free in the world, but she always returns."

As hard as it was for Lucas to hear, it was exactly what he needed. It made him angry, it made him boil and seethe below the surface. It hardened him for what was yet to come.

"If the old man wasn't where he was supposed to be, then I can't help you. Maybe he saw what was going down and bailed out; he never struck me as having much spine. So what else do you need from me?"

"Just a token of appreciation. The accounts that your father had in Banco Baudin were guaranteed to me as a bonus for killing him. I want my money."

"I'm disappointed. For a minute there, I thought you might be a man with principles and purpose. But you're really just a murderer for money," Lucas said.

The smiled vanished from Abd al-Rahman's face. He stood straight and lifted his chin into an arrogant pose like he was about to have his photograph taken standing next to a king. He back-handed Lucas across the mouth. It was just a grazing blow, but his teeth tore the inside of his lips and blood began to seep onto his tongue. He could taste the coppery liquid flowing, but he kept his lips tightly shut and sucked the blood down. He wasn't going to give al-Rahman the pleasure of seeing him bleed.

"My father didn't leave me shit after you killed him. I've got nothing to give you, so go ahead and do your worst, asshole."

"You saw the bodies of the other men in the salon, yes? They didn't want to tell me how to access their accounts either, but in the end, they all did. They could have saved themselves a great deal of pain and gone to heaven cleanly, but they preferred to struggle against the inevitable," al-Rahman said.

He paused, and then leaned down and stared directly into Lucas' eyes, "I've just noticed, you have eyes exactly like your sister. I remember them well. She wailed so pitifully when Farouk shipped her off to the slave market at the Bazaar in Algiers; I was tempted to bid a low price on her myself." He could see the change coming across Lucas' face, "But you'll be reunited with her again very soon."

Lucas screamed; not words or threats, but a guttural howl of pure rage. He twisted and jerked against the ropes that held him to the chair, lunging with such force that it teetered up on two legs, and then he and the chair together fell to the side and landed with a crunch. Abd al-Rahman stood back and laughed. He'd succeeded with his first objective, to make Lucas break his stoic strength and be overcome by emotion. Emotion is the interrogator's best weapon.

"It sounded like you might have broken something in that fall, my friend! I hope it wasn't your shooting hand."

In fact, something *had* broken in the fall. The right leg of the chair had cracked neatly at the base, and Lucas felt his foot, tied to the chair leg, slip free. He concealed it until he had the best opportunity to use it.

Abd al-Rahman laughed again and turned to one of the guards by the door, "Come help me pick him up." The guard smiled and walked over, bent down and grabbed Lucas by the neck and pulled him back upright. The chair clacked as it rocked back onto four legs, then made a loud creak and wobbled.

Abd al-Rahman was standing directly in front of Lucas; he looked at the chair just as Lucas pushed his weight back and with his freed leg, drove his heel just below al-Rahman's kneecap. It folded back, and the exterior ligament let go with a sickening *pop*, like a small balloon being pricked with a pin.

Al-Rahman grabbed his knee and wailed, hopping

sideways to the wall to catch his balance.

Lucas' hidden earpiece suddenly came alive again, and he heard Diggs' crackling voice say, "*Now.*"

The glass window behind the second guard shattered and sprayed across the deck, just as a .338 Lapua bullet tore through the guard's chest and flattened him. At the same instant, Diggs was coming through the door, weapon up. The guard standing next to the chair Lucas was tied to, fumbled to raise his machine gun in a panic; *wham-wham,..wham*; the familiar three-shot assassin's song rang out, and he went down in a heap. Diggs spun quickly to his left and took aim at Abd al-Rahman.

"Hold your fire! He's mine!" Lucas yelled. He was wriggling his legs loose, had one hand slipped free and was untying the other. "That bastard killed my father!"

Diggs kept the red laser hovering on Abd al-Rahman's chest, "This isn't a time for heroics, Lucas."

"This one is personal, Diggs," Lucas answered as he threw off the last of the ropes. He cocked his head to the right, and the pain in his neck intensified to a burning streak that ran down his spine.

The blow to his head had nearly ruptured the disk below his C3 vertebrae, and his spinal cord was swelling. He could feel the loss of sensation beginning in his left foot as it radiated with pins-and-needles, and two fingers on his left hand were numb. Throwing a punch with full power from his shoulders was going to be painful, and if he took one more hard shot to the head it might paralyze him.

Abd al-Rahman was gritting his teeth against the shooting pain in his knee, but he managed a sadistic smile and said, "Let the boy prove how brave he is."

Diggs took two steps backward, but held his aim. Abd al-Rahman straightened and turned to face Lucas, looking for any sign of weakness or injury that he might turn to his advantage. He knew the old agent with the gun trained on his chest wasn't going to miss, and wasn't going to let him leave there alive, so he might as well go out fighting.

IN ALL THE years he spent in the Legion, Lucas had learned the most valuable lesson about combat. There's no such thing as a fair fight. The winner goes home, the loser goes in the ground; it's that simple.

He proved his bravery years ago and his only mission now was to kill the bastard who murdered his father, just as he'd killed the men who took his sister.

This was the purest form of the feud; a vendetta that would only be resolved with blood, and all Abd al-Rahman deserved was an execution. Lucas picked up the MP7 that lay on the floor next to the dead guard, pulled it up to his shoulder and took deliberate aim, and fired a single shot into al-Rahman's forehead.

Chapter Thirty-Three

"I thought I'd lost both of you, for a while," Diggs said. "Serge was unresponsive, and I heard you go down after coming onboard."

"Is Serge alright?" Lucas asked.

A squeaky voice came in over the earpiece com, "I'm fine. A mullah stuck a blade in me, but not deep enough to kill me. I finished him off, but I hit my head on something, and passed out for a little while. I came back to life just as Diggs was coming over the deck of the boat. What happened to the girl, is she alive?" Serge said.

"What girl?" Lucas said.

"Avigail. I saw her get on the boat with Farouk. She's there!"

"Farouk must have snatched her at the airport! I never should have left her!" Lucas yelled. Then he pulled his weapon back up to his shoulder, "We have to finish sweeping the boat, she's here somewhere!"

"She didn't look like she was being kidnapped, Lucas," Serge said.

Diggs reached up and pulled his gun down, and looked into his eyes, "Lucas, she's not here, and neither is Farouk. We need to get off this yacht before the police block off the harbor. We'll take the skiff to the point and Serge will pick us up in the van, just like we planned. Let's get to the villa and I'll explain everything on the way."

As THEY MADE the drive along Ma-1 back to the villa, Diggs told them what had happened, "The Fairhope Group has been monitoring Farouk and his organization for the past year, so we knew he was planning to kill his three other associates and increase his sphere of control. It was actually his partners in Beirut, fundraisers for Hezbollah according to my agency contacts, who prompted him to make the move. It would mean significantly higher revenue streams for waging war against the Israelis, with fewer middlemen to take a cut."

"So those were the bodies I stumbled into on the yacht?" Lucas asked.

"Yes. We didn't see any reason to interfere with a bad guy murdering three other bad guys. It made our job easier."

"What about Farouk and Avi?"

"We've known that Avi was working for Farouk. She's always been with Farouk. He was the one who placed her in the employ of Banco Baudin all those years ago to monitor Jean-Étienne Berger's activities and his clients. She was also involved, at least in a small way, with your sister's abduction, and I'm sure she's the one who let Farouk know that your father was asking questions about the gathering here in Mallorca."

Lucas stared out the window of the van as it twisted its way up the mountain road, "And that's what got him killed."

"We believe so. I'm sorry I couldn't share this with you sooner, but we didn't expect you to become involved with her, or for her to show up here in Mallorca with you. It seems now that she also contacted Farouk as soon as we drove away from the airport, and then told him as much as she knew about our plan of attack. They knew where to hit Serge; and they were waiting for you. At least we're getting all of them in the end."

"How's that? We lost both Avi and Farouk," Lucas said.

"We haven't lost them. At the house last night, while the two of you were occupied, I placed a micro-locator into her bracelet; the one she says she never takes off. I knew if she came back to Farouk, that she would be with him when he left and we could track them both. They slipped over the side and left the harbor in a motor launch."

Then he reached into his gear bag and pulled out a small monitor about the size of a cell phone, and folded out a satellite connection antenna. He turned it on and waited six seconds for it to gain a triangulation from three different satellites, operated by the National Reconnaissance Office, and a red position light began to blink.

He turned it around so that Lucas could see the monitor, "They are eighteen miles offshore, and moving at approximately sixteen knots in a southeasterly heading."

Lucas looked up at Serge, who was driving the van, "Drive faster! We can use the black yacht to catch them!"

Serge turned around in his seat, "We used every drop of fuel to get here, it's empty."

"It's being handled," Diggs interrupted. "Lucas, just trust me. We anticipated this."

Chapter Thirty-Four

THE MEDITERRANEAN SEA

The motor launch came roaring up to the side of the yacht and as the driver suddenly throttled back the engine it pitched forward and then rocked back on its own wave before banging hard against the bumpers that hung over the side of the larger vessel. Farouk was almost knocked off his feet by the impact, "You stupid ass! You nearly threw me into the sea!" he screamed at the boat driver.

The step-up platform was quickly lowered by the deckhands, and Farouk climbed up to the rear deck of the yacht, with Avi following behind him. He was angry and in a hurry to get the big ship underway to Algeria and out of the territorial waters of Mallorca.

"Quickly! Tell the captain to leave now!"

The first mate on the rear deck said, "Your Excellency, we must first raise the motor launch up on the boom and secure it to the side for travel."

"Fuck the motor launch! That idiot driver can take it back to Mallorca; we will retrieve it another time. I want to be underway this very minute!"

"Yes, Your Excellency," he said, and he grabbed the radio from his belt and sent the order to the bridge.

Within moments the captain had throttled up the eighteen-thousand horsepower gas-turbine engine, and the green water behind the stern began to boil. The massive yacht lazily inched forward and picked up speed. It would take almost fifteen minutes to reach the top cruising speed of 20 knots, but the sea was beginning to swell under heavy, dark clouds, and 13 knots would be the best they could do for the first hour.

Farouk stormed across the rear platform to the main doors that led into the open salon. One of his attendants rushed ahead and held the door open. As he reached the door, he turned to see Avi, still standing at the edge of the deck on the rear of the yacht as it surged ahead.

"Avigail! Get in here this instant. Clean yourself and put on proper clothing for dinner. I have a lot of questions for you about the banker, and about this boy, Lucas Martell."

SHE WAS STARING at the hills of Mallorca jutting up from the blue water. Hills that were green and golden and flowered up close; scattered with jagged rocks and alive with sea birds that hovered above the pines that whistled in the eastern breeze. She had spent only two nights on this island, and one of those had been the only truly wonderful night of her life. The only time she had ever experienced anything close to real love. *Was it real? Could it have ever been real love?* She thought to herself.

But even if it was real, it didn't matter any longer. She betrayed him. She did her master's bidding and sent Lucas to a certain death. She had looked into his eyes, and even as she felt the sorrow of what she'd done and wished she could undo it, she still turned away from him and followed Farouk.

The yacht surged forward and the wind swirled around her, lifting her dress above her knees and chilling the back of her neck. She looked around, and saw that Farouk had already disappeared inside the yacht, and the crew had moved inside as well, leaving her completely alone.

Avigail turned again to see the hills of Mallorca, now receding in the blue-gray smoke of the engine. Then she looked down at the emerald green sea, boiling and frothing in angry torment against the spinning blades below the hull. She reached up and pulled the clip from her hair and let it fly loose in the breeze. She wiped a tear from her cheek, stepped forward, and plunged thirty feet into the churning spray.

.   .   .

FAROUK WENT into his private berth and showered, then changed into his casual clothes for dinner; long silk pants and a kaftan robe. An hour later he came into the main salon of the upper deck and called for his attendants, irritated that they were not already waiting to serve him as required. His calls went unanswered. He raised his voice and yelled again, "Why do I not have tea waiting for me? Where is everyone?"

The teak door to the galley opened and a tall slender woman entered the room. She was covered from head to toe in a brilliant purple robe with a matching hijab and a netted veil to hide her face. She stood silently for a moment, and stared unabashedly at Farouk.

"We have given your staff the rest of the night off, Farouk," she said.

She spoke in perfect Arabic, but her accent was strange. Not North African, but with a fluid rhythm more typical of the eastern Arabian peninsula.

Before he could answer, two men came in behind him and seized his arms and twisted them behind his back. He cried out in pain as they drove him down and his knees collided with the hard floor. Then one of the men pulled his head back and rammed an oily engine rag into his mouth to keep him from speaking.

The slender woman stepped forward and in her

left hand she held a long, jeweled dagger with solid gold handles and a glimmering blade. She placed it against Farouk's neck and held it just firmly enough that the razor sharp edge incised his tender pale flesh, and drops of blood began to dribble down his throat.

"I remember your threatening blade, Farouk. And now you will remember mine," she said. "At least, for a short time."

He looked bewildered, confused. His eyes were watering from the pain of being cut, but he couldn't make a sound. He blinked away the tears and stared in disbelief that this was happening to him.

"You don't know who I am, do you Farouk?" she said.

He shook his head defiantly and grunted through the rag. The two men at his sides jerked him back to a submissive cower.

"No one is permitted to see me, but for you, I will make an exception this one time."

The woman reached up and unclasped the veil and let it fall to the side. The first thing Farouk saw was her eyes. Large, magnificent green eyes like Persian emeralds glowing in the low light of the room. Then she pulled back the hijab and her golden hair cascaded out and flowed around her body like a sunlit river of curls.

He looked confused again, but for only a second. Then the truth of what he was facing hit him. He shook his head from side to side as if he didn't believe what he was seeing, and then his anger boiled again and he lurched and strained against the two men.

He was being confronted by a ghost. The ghost of a girl he had stolen and sold so many years ago. One girl of thousands. But none had ever returned, until now; and this one returned for vengeance.

Eliza, the golden-haired girl from Mallorca had come back.

She stared into his eyes and when she saw that he recognized her, she smiled. Then she looked up at her men and gave them instructions, "Roll him up in that beautiful carpet in the center of the room, and let's send him on his way."

The men picked Farouk up, each one grabbing an arm and a leg, and carried him to the carpet. They dropped him on his side and began to push him over, holding the edge of the carpet to catch in the spiral.

As they released their grasp, he flailed and swung at them with his fists, and one of the men slapped him with the back of his hand across his cheek so hard it rocked his head and left a glowing pink mottled welt. He cried out again and covered his face with his hands.

As they started to roll him tightly in the carpet, Eliza kneeled down and pulled the rag from his mouth, "I don't want you to suffocate too quickly, Farouk."

His pleas were muted as the carpet swallowed him into a lumpy coil, like a giant python with a fat little pig wriggling in its belly. They tied a length of rope around the carpet to keep it tight, and carried it out to the deck of the ship.

"You deserve to die a thousand times or more, Farouk. A death for every life you've stolen. But alas, I can only kill you once," Eliza said.

His muffled screams echoed from the end of the carpet as the men raised one end, and let it slip over the side.

Eliza leaned over the rail and watched it plummet into the rolling waves. It bobbed to the surface once, and then vanished into the depths.

She wrapped her arms around her chest, closed her eyes, lifted her head and let the wind blow her long hair back like a golden sail. She had dreamed of this moment for years, and felt the emotion rising from deep inside. It was pleasing, and sensual. It was like the embrace of a lover lost many years ago, who finally returned to take her into his arms. It was a pleasurable killing.

AN HOUR LATER, as lightning crackled overhead in the darkness, the Mediterranean night sky came alive for a few seconds with an enormous fireball. It rose from the belly of the yacht and billowed five-hundred feet up, as the boat shattered into millions of pieces and disappeared from radar.

Chapter Thirty-Five

THE VILLA IN PORT D'ANDRATX

"I think I'd like to have breakfast on the terrace this morning, Louisa. Do you mind?" Lucas asked.

"No bother at all. It's a beautiful morning and the fresh air will be good for you. I will bring you some espresso first. Go sit and enjoy the sea. It looks like green glass this morning all the way to Greece."

"Thank you, Louisa."

Lucas opened the French doors and walked out across the stone terrace. There were large ornately decorated pots along the edge, and a small table in the center with hand painted ceramic tiles depicting a scene from Homer's *The Iliad* on top. Lucas' mother had bought the table when she and Francisco honeymooned on the island of Chios in the Aegean Sea, thirty years ago.

Lucas looked at the raging battle relief and passed

his hand lightly over the glimmering surface. *The world hasn't really changed in ten thousand years*, he thought to himself.

The outer edge of the terrace was surrounded by a stylish concrete balustrade; each of the columns shaped like a fluted urn meant to hold the ashes of the dead. It was painted white and crowned at the corners with clay pots that held young bougainvillea vines, just beginning to bloom.

He walked to the edge and leaned against it, and gazed at the far horizon of the Mediterranean. Celeste blue above and turquoise below, divided by an invisible border that held the two apart.

Then he shifted his eyes downward to the bay of Port d'Andratx and scanned the few sailing yachts anchored in the center of the bay, and the women of summer laying claim to the sandy beach.

He watched them unfurl their giant white towels over the sand, and peel their robes away to reveal bronzed bodies and the faintest rumor of swimwear. He took a deep breath and relaxed, having been freed from the demon that haunted him for so long. He could watch and admire now and still feel a pureness of heart.

The murders of three notorious criminals at the hands of a known Hezbollah assassin and two henchmen of the Lebanese underground, caused quite a stir among the locals and the television and newspaper reporters. They concluded it was a deal that had gone very bad and erupted into swinging swords and blazing gunfire that left no survivors.

The local police chief assured everyone on the island that the culprits had all expired. The only other odd news that week was the discovery of a Moroccan fisherman who had decided to end his own life in the bell tower of the La Seu Cathedral, of all places, by hanging himself with a slender piece of rope attached to the giant iron striker.

Bill Diggs and Serge had left the island two days ago, immediately after the harbor murders. They escaped under the cover of darkness in a yacht that was black as night and faster than anything else in the Mediterranean Sea. They made their way back to Monte Carlo in a scant eleven hours, and anchored her off the coast of Cap-d'Ail on the French Riviera.

Maître Jean-Paul Charpentier had all of the contacts necessary to properly register the boat under the name of her new owner, Monsieur Lucas Martell, and she was christened with a new name across her stern: *Eliza*. She'd be there waiting for Lucas when he was ready for another fast voyage.

Lucas' only regret from the previous week had been the loss of Farouk Kateb. He desperately wanted to take him alive; believing Kateb might hold clues about his sister, and perhaps even about his father. Diggs assured him that Farouk had met his end in the sea that day, but he refused to say more; only that it would all become clear in the end.

At the very least, Lucas felt that he should have been the one to end Farouk's life; to fulfill his duty in the vendetta. Typical for Diggs, he told Lucas to focus on the needs of the moment, not the unimportant details; and the needs of the moment were being here in Mallorca, and beginning his life anew.

SOMETHING in the bay caught his attention. It was a new yacht, much larger than all the others, moored at the outer edge of the deep blue water, but protected from the western winds by the cliffs. It must have been at least three hundred feet in length, with four decks and a helipad over the stern.

Lucas had never seen anything like it here in the small bay. It wasn't there yesterday or the day before, so it must have come in sometime during the night. A very dangerous approach in this narrow bay for a vessel the size of this one. Her captain must be highly skilled, and perhaps he had intimate knowledge of the bay.

They might be regular summer residents. I suppose I'm the real stranger here, he thought to himself.

Louisa came out carrying a silver tray with a small green espresso cup and sugar, and set it down it on the table.

"Louisa, there are binoculars under the cabinet, just inside the door. Would you mind grabbing them for me?" Lucas asked, not taking his eyes off the yacht.

She smiled and nodded, and returned a moment later with them in hand.

Lucas raised the binoculars to his eyes, adjusted the focusing ring with his right thumb and looked intently at the massive vessel, scanning from bow to stern and automatically committing the details to memory.

By the shape and design it was likely built by Blohm & Voss in the Netherlands. Only a few shipbuilders in the world create private mega yachts of this size and caliber, and only a handful of people in the world can afford them; the mega-rich of the rich.

It had a deep long chine in the bow for breaking ocean sized waves, and he could see full radar navigation equipment mounted above the bridge. She was built to navigate the oceans of the world at will.

He counted seven deck hands working above, which meant there were likely twenty more on staff below to operate and maintain the vessel and serve the passengers. But who were the passengers?

"Louisa, can you recall seeing that large yacht before, here in the bay?" he asked.

Louisa walked up to the edge of the terrace and held her hand above her brow and squinted her eyes as she looked out across the water.

"I couldn't say for certain, Lucas. I don't pay

much attention to the boats, and they all look very much the same to me."

"That one doesn't look anything like the others, Louisa. It's enormous. Are you sure?"

"I can't say, but it looks as though it might belong to someone very important, doesn't it?" she said. "I'll be back out with your breakfast in a just a few minutes."

Lucas continued watching as the deck crew pulled the canvas cover off a twenty-foot motor launch and lowered it over the side with a hydraulic winch. The driver started the engine and pulled it around to the rear boarding deck, where another passenger stepped into the launch and took a seat under the sun awning, as it powered up and came towards the shore.

As the launch beached itself directly onto the white sand, Lucas could see the two occupants more clearly through the binoculars. The driver was a tall man, dark skinned, and well dressed. He was wearing neatly pressed slacks and deck sandals, a tailored white shirt, and a light summer jacket.

The driver jumped from the bow of the boat onto the beach, and as his jacket tightened around his midsection, Lucas saw the unmistakable outline of a weapon in a shoulder holster tucked under his arm.

Lucas reached into the front pocket of his slacks and wrapped his fingers around the grip of a stainless steel Walther PPK; a parting gift from Diggs. He said it would handle the salty air better than the H&K,

and it was easily concealed in summer clothes on the island.

He looked down and pulled the slide back half an inch to confirm the shiny brass cartridge in the chamber; levered the safety to OFF, and slid it back in his pocket.

Maybe it was just coincidence that what appeared to be two Arabs or North Africans had arrived only days after Lucas had killed a score of the them, but he didn't want to take any chances.

He raised the binoculars again to see the second occupant standing on the bow of the launch, it was obviously a woman. He believed she was slender, but her clothes made it difficult to tell. She was wearing a loose-fitting dress and a pale green wrap that wound around her body from her shoulders to her shins, and a scarf that covered her head and neck and her lower chin. Large dark sunglasses covered any other view of her face.

The boat driver waded ankle-deep into the lapping waves and carried her from the bow to the dry sand, setting her gently down on her feet, then bowing to her submissively.

The pair began to walk across the beach to the path that came up to the villa, the woman leading, the man following. As they reached the stone path, Lucas lost sight of them in the Aleppo pines.

He moved to the side gate of the terrace, where the path would lead the pair, and he stood next to the concrete column that could shield him if needed. He could hear the echo in the trees of their sandals lightly crunching over gravel as they neared. They were not trying to mask their approach.

The woman came into view first, and she froze as rigid as a statue when she saw Lucas standing at the gate. He was gripping the Walther with the gun half drawn from the shelter of his trousers.

The woman turned her head and raised her hand to the man following, and he stopped behind her. She whispered something to him, and he bowed his head and took three steps back down the path. Lucas returned the pistol back to his pocket, and relaxed his shoulders.

The woman reached up slowly and pulled the tucked-in end of her scarf free and began to unwind it. Slowly around her neck first, then the second loop around exposed the milky skin of her forehead, and as the scarf fell loose on the third pass, her long, golden hair came with it. She pulled the glasses from her face and revealed the only other thing Lucas needed to identify her. Eyes as green as the emerald sea.

His knees buckled slightly, and he caught himself with a hand on the gate. His breath hung in his throat and he stood completely transfixed. Surely she was a specter. A phantom come to haunt him. He forced himself to breath deeply but he couldn't speak.

"Hello, Lucas," Eliza said.

They both took three quick steps forward and

threw their arms around each other.

"I had to see you. But I can't stay here long …," she said.

THE STORY of Eliza being sold in the Bazaar in Algiers was a lie. The truth was just as sinister, but in the end, had allowed Eliza to survive and thrive when most young girls who are taken did not. Eliza had the misfortune of matching precisely what a Sultan in a small country on the Arabian Peninsula was seeking as a companion for his young son, who was barely older than she. Farouk Kateb had taken her to present as a gift.

The first several years of her enslavement were a torment, and it was all she could do just to survive. At the age of sixteen, she became a consort to the Sultan's son, and no other woman would ever hold his eye again. She felt her hold over him strengthen, and her power in the royal court grew.

Three years ago, the old king had died very suddenly, and his son, Eliza's lover, became the new Sultan. Eliza was granted the title of Chief Consort to the Sultan, and at twenty-years-old she became the most powerful woman in the country. Once she had power, she began to think of revenge.

"FOR YEARS, I could hear your voice calling my name. I knew you were trying to save me," she said.

Lucas bent over in the chair and put his face in his hands, remembering that day and his failure, "I'm so sorry, Eliza."

"Don't be sorry, Lucas. We can't change the past, and my life isn't difficult anymore."

"At least it's finally over," he said.

"No, Lucas. This is just the beginning."

"The beginning of what?" he asked

"There are others out there, Lucas. Many others who are part of the evil in this world. They steal children and sell them into slavery, they trade drugs and guns, and wage wars with the profits. Farouk Kateb was just a very small fish in a sea of monsters. Abd al-Rahman, the assassin that you killed, wasn't just working for Farouk. He had a different master; someone we haven't found yet. We think he might have actually been the one who plotted the deaths of all the brokers, and maybe even led you down the path to kill Berger. Right after you left Monte Carlo, someone took control of all of Banco Baudin's assets and clients, and we think they're trying to gain control of the entire human trafficking market in this hemisphere."

Then she added, "I want you to take charge of Fairhope Group."

"What do you know about Fairhope?"

"I've been funding it from the very beginning,

Lucas. I have access to unlimited resources. I just needed someone capable of hunting and killing evil men. I found Diggs first, and then six months ago he found out you were fighting in the French Foreign Legion. Imagine my surprise."

"So that's what he meant by 'interview'," Lucas said.

"Lucas, between the two of us, we can tear their little world down, piece by piece."

THE DAY PASSED TOO QUICKLY for brother and sister, having been apart so many years. Eliza held Lucas for a long time at the top of the hill, then kissed his cheek, and told him that she would be in contact again, very soon. She and her guard departed the same way they came, and he watched them on the launch as they motored back to the massive yacht.

As he watched through the binoculars and raised his hand to wave, he saw something else unexpected. Another woman standing on the forward deck. She was wearing gray capri pants and a white blouse that contrasted with her long dark hair. When he waved, she waved back.

The tracking device that Diggs had planted in Avi's bracelet had done more than give them the location of Farouk's yacht. It had saved her life. Eliza's crew had plucked her from the sea.

She confessed to Eliza everything that she had

done, and how she came to be in the service of Farouk Kateb. Eliza took pity on her, but thought it best not to let Lucas know that she was alive. At least not yet.

As it turned out, her knowledge of Farouk and his Hezbollah partners was of great interest to the Israeli Mossad, and given that Avi had been stolen from her home country as a child, they welcomed her back.

The next morning when he rose and stepped out onto the terrace, the massive yacht was gone, having slipped away in the night as quietly as it arrived. Lucas reached into his shirt pocket and pulled out the shiny silver flash drive that Jean-Étienne Berger had loaded with endless information about the corrupt men and companies that funneled money through his bank.

He held it up and it glinted from the orange morning sunlight filtering through the pines. What he held in the tip of his fingers was the power to turn the world upside-down. The power to reach across the chasm to the world behind this world, to the men who thought of themselves as gods.

And then he knew what he was going to do. He was going to hunt them down, one by one, and kill them all. He was going to bring such pain to the world of these evil men that Satan himself would openly weep for their pitiful souls.

What Did You Think?

Thank you for reading **Mallorca Vendetta**.

If you liked it, I have a favor to ask. Like all other authors these days, my success depends entirely on you. Your opinions and thoughts about the book are all that matter. People want to know what you think.

Please, take a minute and share your thoughts in a brief review. You can help make this book a success.

Just sign in to your Amazon account, go to the sales page for **Mallorca Vendetta**, and click the button that says (**Write a Review**) near the bottom of the page.

Thank You!

Also by William Jack Stephens

Coming October 2019!

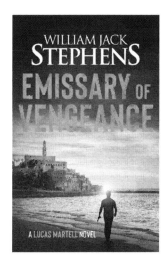

Book 2 of the Lucas Martell Series. Everyone on my mailing list will receive advanced notice of discounts!

Get connected with me here: **Mailing List Sign Up**

Or sign up at my website: www.williamjackstephens.com

Also by William Jack Stephens

Andalusian Legacy

A Daring Escape...Murder...Revenge.

A Spanish Crime Lord... Young lovers trapped in the Criminal Underworld...

Where The Green Star Falls

Barely a Whisper Separates The Living From the Lost...

Blending wisdom, mysticism, and real-life drama into an inspirational saga of self-discovery, Where The Green Star Falls is quickly becoming a modern classic, and transforming the lives of readers around the world.

About the Author

Jack has lived and explored the world from the Arctic to the southern reaches of Patagonia, and now splits his time between Atlanta in the USA, and a house in the Andes Mountains of southern Argentina.

In his former life, he served in executive roles with some of the largest companies in the world. He interacted with government agents, gave private industry counseling to congressional leaders, and served on committees that planned for nuclear, biological, or chemical disaster.

Now he writes gripping thrillers, tales of adventure, and the occasional love story.

www.williamjackstephens.com

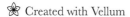

Printed in Great Britain
by Amazon